BACKWOODS

ALSO BY BRANDON MASSEY

BACKWOODS

BRANDON MASSEY

DARK CORNER PUBLISHING

THE CALLING

L ater that autumn evening, after her last free ride had dropped her off somewhere outside of Macon, Georgia, the runaway teenage girl was shuffling along the grassy shoulder of the desolate country road, trying to decide where she would sleep for the night, when she heard what sounded like an amusement park.

The unexpected noises brought her to a sudden halt in the tangled weeds.

Am I going crazy? Am I really hearing this?

She pivoted to the right. A deep, dark forest lay beyond the road and seemed to stretch on forever. Straightening her backpack across her shoulders, she tilted her head, listening.

The noises were faint, but not a hallucination: the rollicking music of a pipe organ . . . joyous cries of children on whirring theme park rides . . . the clank and clatter of fun machines . . .

There were fragrant, delicious smells, too, brief notes of them wafting on the warm breeze: sweet funnel cakes, juicy hot dogs, giant baked pretzels, crispy French fries.

Her mouth watered.

Was it a carnival? She'd been to such a place once, as a younger child, during happier times in her family, before things fractured. She had warm memories of screaming gleefully on park rides with her cousins and gorging herself on delectable treats until her stomach felt ready to burst.

As if her feet had a will of their own, she left the roadside and wandered deeper into the woods.

Some instinctive part of her flashed a warning, told her that danger lay ahead, but her sensory impressions of the spectacle awaiting her blew away those red flags. The carnival sounds grew louder; the smells, stronger.

And she glimpsed, through the pine trees, the unmistakable sight of a Ferris wheel, lit up against the dusky sky.

Oh my goodness! It really is *a carnival!*

She broke into a run, stamping through weeds, knocking aside branches and vines.

After she had sprinted for maybe a hundred yards, she reached a towering chain-link fence, the top of it festooned with glistening coils of barbed wire. The formidable barrier extended as far as she could see, on both left and right.

She was set to turn away, despite the deep craving that gripped her pounding heart. Although she was nimble, and had taken gymnastics classes as a little girl, there was no vaulting over what was probably a ten-foot-high fence.

Gnawing her bottom lip, she ran her slender brown fingers along the cool chain links. So close, but so far away. The enchanting music throbbed in her ears, the tempting smells were so near she could literally taste the food, and the glimmering Ferris wheel lay just beyond a rise in the gentle, forested hills.

On her left, she noticed a gap in the fence—like a patch had been cut out, especially for her. It seemed to shimmer in the moonlight, like a magical portal.

It hadn't been there before. Had it?

Of course it was, silly. You just didn't notice it, because it's almost full dark.

2

She edged toward the opening.

Don't go in there, a stern voice whispered in the back of her mind. A familiar voice—her mother's.

But her mother was mostly to blame for her running away from home in the first place. Listening to Mom had brought her only misery.

She shrugged off the warning, bent slightly, and stepped across the threshold . . .

1

What began as a perfect morning for Nick Alexander went sideways quickly, and in hindsight, what hurt the most was that it was his own damned fault.

At sunrise, he was making love to his girlfriend, Amiya, their bodies joined in a sweet grinding on his Chinese sleigh bed in his Atlanta home. It had started as breakfast in bed—bagels and coffee Nick fetched from a café in his Buckhead neighborhood—but had evolved with unexpected speed into them grasping for each other with a desperate hunger that had surprised him. They had been together all night and had made love for hours before finally falling asleep, and still, they couldn't get enough of each other.

Straddling him, Amiya rocked in a seductive rhythm, her curly ebony hair hanging down her face in a veil, her lithe figure gyrating, sunlight glistening on her smooth, dark brown skin. His hands roamed alternately between her waist and her hips. Eyes closed, matching her rhythm with his thrusts, he thought with sudden clarity that there was nowhere he would have rather been, and in his forty years on Earth, he had been almost everywhere.

"Do you love me, baby?" she asked, flicking her hair away with her slender fingers.

"Yeah," he said, short of breath. "Yeah, yeah. All day long."

"You want us to have some babies?"

"Yeah, for sure." He grunted. "All right, yeah . . ."

"You want me to marry you?"

"Yeah . . . wait." His eyes flew open. "What?"

"Gotcha." She smiled down at him, bent lower, kissed him.

He ran his fingers down her smooth back and clutched her against him. Soon after, an orgasm buckled through them, leaping between them like an electrical current. They collapsed together on the mattress, limbs entangled, chests pressed together, hearts beating so closely Nick couldn't tell which throbbing belonged to him or her.

April sunshine slanted through the partially opened Venetian blinds and painted stripes on the walls. Nick could hear birds singing and the sighing of the spring breeze. Although his six-bedroom home was in the throbbing heart of Buckhead, the morning was so peaceful they might have been on vacation at a bed-and-breakfast cottage deep in the countryside.

"You shouldn't play like that, you know," he said.

"Play like what?" Amiya lifted her head off his bare chest and gazed at him. Her brown eyes, flecked with amber, glimmered with amusement.

"The marriage thing. You know how important that is to me. How I want the whole package."

"Sweetheart, I'm not a toy in a box delivered by FedEx," Amiya said. "One of multiple items in your Amazon shipment."

"You know what I mean."

"Let's not ruin the moment." She punctuated her request with a soft kiss. "One day at a time, Nick."

Nick had proposed to her a month ago at Bacchanalia, a French restaurant where they'd had their first date sixteen months ago. Flustered, Amiya had declined the three-carat diamond engagement ring with the response that she had to "think about it." Nick pocketed the ring and resumed dinner as if he'd never asked.

He hadn't expected Amiya to immediately say "yes." He'd wanted to gauge her reaction, to get a handle on how close she might be to taking his hand. Checking the temperature of the relationship was how he thought of it. He was getting hot, but needed to crank things up a few more degrees.

He wanted to marry her, obviously. Thirty-three years old, she was gorgeous and smart. She held a PhD in psychology and put those brains to use as an associate professor at Clark Atlanta University, and a part-time counselor. She came from a family of means—both of her parents were highly specialized physicians—but she moved easily in social circles across the spectrum.

They had shared interests, too. One rainy weekend, they stayed in and binge-watched episodes of *Stranger Things* on Netflix. Most important of all, his mother adored her.

She checked all the boxes on his list. That wouldn't have been an issue if she hadn't realized that he *had* a list and had measured her against it, that he was assessing her suitability to complement the other things he had accomplished in his life: the whole package, he liked to call it.

He had money in abundance, thanks to his booming nutritional supplements company. He had the swanky Buckhead home, a trio of luxury vehicles, and the admiration of the community.

But he didn't have Amiya.

She kissed him again, a soul-stirring kiss that started to arouse him all over again. When he reached for her, she slipped out of bed.

"I've got to go make the donuts, baby," she said. "So do you."

"I'm the boss. I get to the office whenever I damn well please."

"Nice, but I don't have it like that. I have students waiting on me and a department head breathing down my neck if I don't show."

"You could say goodbye to all of that if we got married. You wouldn't have to work."

She smiled. "We'll resume this discussion another time."

While she showered and dressed, he sat up in bed, sipping coffee and watching CNN on the sixty-inch flat-screen TV hanging on the wall. Watching the news depressed him and felt like a waste of time, and he had other, more productive activities he could pursue.

He slipped on his running gear. He saw Amiya off to work, with her promising to come by that evening, and as she pulled out of his driveway in her Honda Accord coupe, he hit the road adjacent to his home.

He had an athletic club membership, but there was nothing like running outdoors, breathing in the fresh, flower-scented air, and challenging himself with the shifting terrain of the streets in his own neighborhood.

He had jogged for half a mile when he became aware that a vehicle was following him. He looked over his shoulder.

"Oh, shit," he said.

A gleaming black Cadillac Escalade trailed him, perhaps thirty feet behind. The windows were tinted smoke-black, but Nick didn't have to look inside to find out the identity of the primary occupant.

He briefly considered running, discarded the thought as foolish. Running would have only made things worse.

Running might have gotten him killed.

The driver tapped the horn.

Nick stopped in his tracks. The SUV pulled alongside him. The rear passenger door swung open.

"Nick," a familiar voice said, deep as a black hole. "Get in, my brother. We've got important business to discuss."

2

Four people occupied the big SUV's three rows. There was the driver, some bald steroid freak bursting out of his blue muscle shirt, a serpent tattoo writhing from underneath his collar and wrapping around the back of his head. A bronze-skinned woman rode shotgun. She also had a shaved head, and Nick saw multiple tattoos adorning her neck and shoulders.

The ebony-hued Black man sitting in the rear passenger row had summoned Nick to the vehicle. Nick knew him; his name was Shango. Nick didn't know his last name; he didn't *want* to know it. Rumor had it that Shango's birth name was something ordinary like Dwayne Taylor, and that he'd changed his name to Shango because that was the name of an African god, and he believed he had a divine destiny.

In the middle row in front of Shango, occupying the seat like a kid stuck in after-school detention, sat Nick's business partner, Omar Reeves.

Omar looked terrified: his face filmed with greasy sweat and dark eyebrows twitching. But he didn't speak, merely inclining his head toward Nick.

Moving on feet that felt loaded with sandbags, Nick climbed into the vehicle and sat on the rear seat that Shango patted as if calling a puppy to heel.

The inside of the truck smelled of marijuana, the scent so cloying that it made it even harder for Nick to breathe. That was saying something because the fear lodged in his windpipe threatened to asphyxiate him.

Shango wore a charcoal two-piece suit, black shirt, and expensive Italian loafers. He was bald, but had a thick, longish beard tapered to a fine point.

Shango's obsidian eyes took in everything and gave nothing back. He stared at Nick, silent, until Nick broke eye contact.

"Let's roll," Shango said. He had the ghost of a Brooklyn accent, but Nick knew little about the man's roots.

As the Escalade cruised out of his neighborhood, Shango took a long draw from a vape pen and expelled smoke from his nostrils like a dragon.

Nick suppressed a cough. "Where are we going?"

Shango didn't answer, didn't look at him. He pulled an iPhone out of his jacket and tapped text messages.

"Can I use my phone, too?" Nick asked.

"Why would you want to do that, brother?" Shango grinned at him through a plume of smoke. "To call the police? To contact perhaps your beautiful girlfriend, Amiya Turner, who is heading toward work now at her college? Or your mother, Valerie Alexander, who is most likely watering her flowers on her front porch now?"

Nick tried to conceal the chill that washed over him. "Never mind."

He wanted to strangle Omar. Omar, his old Morehouse room-mate, had hooked them up with Shango two years ago. Shango had supplied venture capital (in the loosest sense of the term) for their then-fledgling nutritional supplements company, in return for a percentage of profits.

But you didn't make a deal with the devil and expect to emerge unscathed. Nick had felt uncomfortable allowing a man of Shango's questionable reputation to back their business, but when the banks had declined to extend loans, when their credit cards had been maxed out, and when their relatives had pleaded empty pockets, he found himself justifying how a deal with the man could work to their advantage. *Just pay him his percentage and keep him out of our business.*

Since their agreement, they had been paying Shango, on time, every month, and Shango had kept his distance. Nick was only minimally involved in their business accounting—he left the business operations to Omar while he focused on product development—but for his own peace of mind, he reviewed Shango's payments. That monthly royalty check to "Divine Inspirations," the ridiculous sham business Shango used, got cut before they even paid the rent on their warehouse.

Nick's best guess for the purpose of this "discussion" was that Shango wanted new terms.

The Escalade crawled south along the Downtown Connector. It was eight o'clock in the morning, near the peak of Atlanta's notoriously awful rush-hour traffic. Wherever they were headed, it was going to take a while to get there.

"What's this impromptu meeting all about?" Nick asked. "Since we're stuck in traffic, can we have the discussion now? The gang's all here, right?" He offered a light chuckle.

Shango lifted his index finger to his lips in the universal gesture for silence. "You could use one of those Cool Breeze pills right now, brother."

Cool Breeze was one of the dietary supplements in their product line. Utilizing a "proprietary blend of naturally sourced herbs," it promised to soothe the consumer's spirit and bestow an overall sense of well-being with daily use.

It was a specious claim, Nick knew. None of their products had ever been tested in a lab for efficacy. Such testing wasn't required; the Food and Drug Administration didn't regulate nutritional supplements as they did prescription drugs. Companies such as Nick's operated in a nebulous world of outrageous claims, slick advertising, and mysterious "proprietary" blends. Anyone could manufacture some pills, toss them in a bottle, and start selling them online, and that happened more often than most people realized.

But Nick held a doctorate in chemistry from Emory University and had worked as a researcher for a major pharmaceuticals firm for almost a decade. He knew what he was doing; his formulations *should* have worked, at least to a degree, based on current science. But there was a chasm, a huge one, between the promises and the actual product. There had to be. The competitive nature of the industry demanded it.

There was too much damned money to be made to risk telling the truth.

Consumers wanted to believe in a magic pill to help them shed pounds. They wanted a powder to help them "get ripped," clamored for products to improve their mental focus, and wished for a natural solution to erectile dysfunction. Nick gave people what they wanted, and if the science wasn't a hundred percent legit, it was *mostly* there, and the placebo effect would fill in the rest.

That was what he told himself. That was how he slept well at night.

What did occasionally wake him in the wee hours of the morning was the possibility that, one day, he would be riding to an unknown destination with a man like Shango beside him.

3

Nick had been fearful that they were traveling to an abandoned warehouse, a remote field, a desolate edge of the Chattahoochee River—all the clichéd places that, in the movies, gangsters such as Shango employed to execute victims and dump the dead bodies.

But they drove only to their company's headquarters in South Atlanta. They rented office space in a corporate park less than five miles away from Hartsfield-Jackson Atlanta International Airport.

"You could have set a meeting with us here at the office," Nick said. "You didn't need to pick us up."

Shango only smiled. It wasn't a pleasant expression, and Nick had a pretty good idea of the intent behind it: Shango had picked them up because he wanted them to understand that he could get to them, anywhere, whenever he wanted.

"Let's go inside," Shango said, and opened his door.

Legacy Nutrition operated with a lean crew, either independent contractors who came to the offices only when required, or resources provided by third-party vendors. Customer service reps in the Philippines attended to their toll-free customer service number around the clock, taking orders, answering emails that came in via their website, and logging the occasional complaint. Their products were manufactured in China. Product was stored in a climate-controlled facility a few miles away and distributed by a vendor that took a small cut of sales. Usually, the only personnel in the office were a couple of assistants who performed basic administrative functions, both of whom were relatives of Omar and worked flexible, part-time hours.

Omar unlocked the door to the office. Shango's driver waited behind in the vehicle, but the woman who'd been riding shotgun came with them.

Exotically beautiful—Nick guessed she was biracial, with Asian and African American parentage—she was as tall as Nick, about five-ten. She wore black leggings and a tight-fitting orange tank top that showed off a pair of arms more muscular than Nick's.

"Why do I feel as if I've seen you before?" Nick said.

"That's how it is?" She sneered. "You'll have to come at me better than that if you wanna get these panties off, honey."

"That's not what I meant." Nick blushed. "I'm serious. I've seen you somewhere before."

"If you've ever followed mixed martial arts, you might have seen Wanda," Shango said. "She was a women's heavyweight champion five years back: Wanda the Wonderful. Her specialty is Muay Thai."

Wanda grinned at him and pantomimed an elbow strike.

"Oh," Nick said. "That would explain why I recognized you. I casually follow MMA."

Omar led them to the conference room off the main carpeted corridor, and switched on the overhead lighting. The room was furnished with only the basics: a long conference table, plastic swivel chairs, a small side table that held a conference telephone, and a vase of silk carnations.

Shango took the seat at the head of the table and beckoned for them to sit around him. Wanda stood on the other side of the room and watched them with a serpent's slitted gaze.

"I see business is going well," Shango said. He swept his arm around them. "You've got modest digs here, but that's cool. Outside of here, though, both of you brothers have been ballin'." Grinning like a shark, Shango glanced at Omar. "You bought that crib in Sandy Springs for one point three, from what I read."

"It didn't cost that much," Omar said.

"Yes." Shango raised his finger. "One point three mill. Seven cars, too. One for each day of the week, am I right? Are we big pimpin' now, brother?"

"Damn, Omar," Nick said. "*Seven* cars?"

"So?" Omar glared at him. "I work hard; we both do. We deserve to reap the rewards."

"I agree," Shango said. "*We* deserve to reap the rewards." He shifted to Nick. "Now you. Nine hundred large for the swanky pad in Buckhead. You don't have seven cars, but you've got three: a Bentley, a Ferrari, a Range Rover. And let's not forget, a brand-new Honda Pilot for your moms."

"And?" Nick shrugged. "I don't apologize for that."

"My brothers, I've got to increase my royalty to thirty percent." Shango clasped his hands together and swept his gaze across them. "We got a deal?"

The bottom had dropped out of Nick's stomach, as if he'd been pushed over a cliff. He couldn't find any words in response. But Omar erupted out of his seat so violently that his chair toppled to the carpet.

"Thirty percent is extortion!" Omar said. "That's twice what we're giving you now!"

"Indeed," Shango said. He steepled his fingers. "I thought it was fair. I have only two vehicles. I'll have to ask for thirty-five percent now."

"Whoa," Nick said. "Come on, man. Be reasonable."

"Forty," Shango said. He grinned.

"Is this a joke?" Omar asked. "Because you're out of your mind."

"Forty-five." Shango cracked his knuckles.

Nick felt dizzy. He grabbed the edges of the table as if to balance himself. Omar was the numbers guy, but Nick knew their costs. At a forty-five percent royalty, off the top, that would leave Nick and Omar with only twenty percent to themselves, after expenses. Shango had cut their profits by more than half in a matter of minutes.

"No goddamn way," Omar said. "No deal."

Shango tilted his head toward Wanda. The woman smiled and sauntered around the table toward Omar.

Nick tensed, but Omar glared at her. He was six-two and in shape.

"You don't scare me, bitch," Omar said. "Back off."

The blow came so fast that Nick hadn't seen it coming. Wanda slammed her elbow into Omar's face, and Nick heard something crunch. Omar gasped and staggered forward on watery legs. Wanda looped her arms around his neck, jerked him forward, and rammed her knee deep into his kidney. Omar let out a garbled squeak. Wanda released him, and he collapsed like a limp doll to the floor.

"Who's the bitch now?" Wanda glared at Omar as he writhed on the floor. She swiveled toward Nick. "You want some, too, little man?"

"No, ma'am." Trembling, Nick shook his head.

"It's fifty percent now, family," Shango said. He rubbed his hands together like a man anticipating a sumptuous meal. "Oh, and I'll take a reasonable cash advance, too."

4

The "reasonable cash advance" that Shango had casually required was for the entirely unreasonable sum of 1.5 million dollars.

Shango and his crew of goons had left. Omar hunched over the sink in the office restroom, spitting blood into the basin and tenderly assessing his bruised face. Standing in the doorway, Nick had tried to talk Omar into going to the hospital. His partner's jaw had to be dislocated, possibly broken, and he was probably going to be pissing blood for a few days.

Omar was less interested in his health and more concerned about coming up with Shango's money, and Nick tended to agree with him. Shango had not set a date for when he expected payment, but Nick doubted that the guy had a reputation for patience.

"How much do we have in cash reserves?" Nick asked. "We should be able to cover it, right? I mean, it's gonna hurt for sure, but don't we have the funds?"

Omar pressed a wet towel against his face that he had filled with ice cubes, a makeshift ice pack. Wincing, he said, "Not as much as he's asking for."

"But how much?" Nick asked.

"About a hundred." Omar didn't meet his gaze.

"A hundred thousand dollars?" Nick couldn't believe what he had heard. "Omar, we're bringing in what—almost a million a month, gross sales? But we have only a hundred grand in savings?"

"We've got expenses, Nick. It's not that simple. We gotta pay all these vendors: the phone reps, the office space, the manufacturing company in Beijing. We've got employees and contractors. We pay ourselves, too, serious coin."

"I didn't know you had seven cars," Nick said.

"I'm supposed to tell you every time I buy a car?"

Nick turned away from the bathroom, paced across the adjoining hallway. Beads of cold sweat pebbled his hairline.

"I've got about fifty grand in savings," Nick said. "What about you?"

Omar was shaking his head. "I don't know, about five, I guess."

"Five thousand dollars in savings? And yet you own seven luxury vehicles?"

"What are you, my dad?" Omar spat blood on the carpet between them. "I could sell the cars—it still won't be enough. I'd net maybe four hundred. You could sell yours, too. What would we get?"

Nick did some quick math in his head. "Two fifty, rough guess."

"All right, three hundred from you—that includes your savings. Four hundred from me. A hundred in the company cash fund, a total of eight hundred grand. He wants one point five. We're still short seven hundred."

"Jesus." Nick slumped against the wall. "What about a loan?"

"A loan?"

"A bank loan. We've got business credit; we have Amex cards for both of us in the business name. Why not go to the bank?"

"I can look at that, but realistically I don't see a bank fronting us seven hundred, Nick. We're still a new business, not much of a credit history, and we don't have A1 credit, not as Legacy Nutrition. You know how tight it was when we got started. Robbing Peter to pay Paul like my moms would say."

Nick remembered those lean days, when leaving his cushy job with a pharmaceuticals firm to start his own company had seemed like a catastrophic mistake. "Okay, I know it's a long shot. But do you think Shango might negotiate?"

Omar actually laughed, though a spark of pain flashed in his eyes and he cradled his face. "Yeah, like he *negotiated* his royalty from fifteen percent to fifty?"

"Why do you think he wants all this cash from us anyway?" Nick asked. "Why isn't the royalty hike enough? Why hit us up for more?"

"Maybe because he's a criminal, Nick?" Omar spat again, pressed the ice pack to his swollen jaw. "He sees our business making money hand over fist, and in his mind, it's like an ATM. He's gonna suck out cash whenever he wants."

"You knew this about him but thought he was a good choice as an investor for us?" Nick said.

"I didn't know what I know now, okay?" Omar found a chair, nearly collapsed into it. Nick found a nearby chair, settled into that one.

They hung their heads in silence.

"What do you think he'll do if we don't pay him the full amount?" Nick asked. "What if we give him what we can, up front, and then go on a payment plan for the balance?"

"He's not the IRS, man. Guys like him don't do payment plans."

"But we need to be sure. We need to ask him. *You* need to ask him. He's your contact."

Icepack cradled against his face, Omar closed his eyes and tilted his head backward, resting it against the wall behind him. He sighed.

"Ask him," Nick said.

"Don't expect miracles," Omar finally said.

5

Nick took an Uber back to his house. There, he showered, changed clothes, and drove to visit his mother in Roswell.

He had already talked to his mom on the phone, but after Shango had mentioned his mother by name, with specific descriptions of her usual daytime activities, Nick felt a compulsive urge to see her in the flesh to ensure she was okay and hadn't been touched by the nightmare that had invaded his life.

He had checked on Amiya, too, and confirmed via text that she was fine, busy at work, and would be coming over that evening.

Nick didn't plan on telling either his mom or Amiya, the two most important people in his life, what was going on in his business dealings with Shango. He had never disclosed his ties to the crime lord to anyone. The less anyone knew, the better; if any of these misdeeds ever wound up in a criminal court, the women he loved would be indisputably innocent.

His mom was a retired accountant and lived in a cozy, three-bedroom townhome in Roswell. She had moved into the house four years ago, after his dad had died of a heart attack at the age of sixty-five.

At eleven o'clock in the morning on a Tuesday, Nick found her sitting in a padded chair on the wooden deck at the back of the house. Flowers in early spring bloom surrounded her. She was drinking iced herbal tea and reading a paperback mystery novel.

"Oh, to enjoy the lazy life of a retiree." Nick leaned down to give her a hug.

"Lazy life, my butt." She removed her glasses and massaged the bridge of her nose. "Tax season just ended. I'm taking a well-deserved break."

"You're supposed to be retired, Mom. Why are you still doing taxes for people?"

"Some folks at the church needed guidance." She gave him a level look. "I do it because I can."

It was a familiar answer from her, one of those mottos that she and his dad had preached to him for his entire life. *Get good grades because you can. Do the right thing because you can.*

Research cures for diseases because you can, Nicholas.

Nick's original calling to medicine had been a mission to find a cure for sickle-cell anemia. The disease had claimed the life of his mother's eldest sister, his beloved Aunt Doris. Although he had been only a teenager at the time of his aunt's passing, the pain that his family had experienced as she wasted away had made an indelible impression on him. He'd always had a knack for science and math, and the pursuit of a degree in the sciences had seemed like a way to make a difference, to perhaps spare someone else's family the pain that his own had endured.

The cause was just, but the money, to him, was never good enough. He'd gotten a doctorate, worked as a pharmaceutical scientist for one of the world's top drug companies, and though he'd done important work, it seemed that the bulk of the financial rewards always went to the company's top executives. It had forced him to face an unpleasant truth about himself: he'd yearned to make a difference with his knowledge, but more than that, he wanted to be rich.

It seemed almost sinful to admit it, given his church upbringing, but the pull of materialism was too strong for him to resist. He wanted to spin around town in expensive cars. He wanted a big house in a tony neighborhood. He wanted a Rolex on his wrist, fine wines in his cellar, and the latest fashionable clothes and shoes waiting in his closet. His respectable but modestly paying corporate gig would never have brought the financial rewards that he craved.

When Omar, his frat brother from Morehouse, had called with a business proposition to launch their own nutritional supplements company, the timing couldn't have been better. Nick had been ready to stake his claim on his own fortune.

"Is everything doing okay, Mom?" Nick settled on a chair next to her.

"I'm doing fine, Nicholas. I'm a little surprised that you're visiting me on a Tuesday morning instead of working. Is everything okay with *you*?" Her gaze probed him.

"I'm all right." He couldn't bear to meet his mother's copper-brown eyes, and looked instead at the menagerie of potted plants assembled on the deck. "Everything is everything."

"All right, then." She pursed her lips, clearly displeased but not willing to push it. "How's Amiya?"

"She's fine. Any day now, I'll pop the question."

Nick hadn't told his mother that he had already asked Amiya to marry him and had gotten a noncommittal response. No good would come of sharing such information with his mother. His mom was crazy about Amiya, but she would side with him and wonder what was wrong with his girlfriend, and he didn't want to give his mother any reason to harbor a negative opinion of her. Amiya would come around, in time.

Yeah, she'll really want to marry you if she finds out a crime boss has you on a string.

"You got any more of that tea?" Nick asked.

"I brewed a whole pitcher. It's in the refrigerator. Help yourself."

In the kitchen, Nick took the glass pitcher of iced tea out of the refrigerator and placed it on the granite-topped island. He wasn't one to snoop around his mother's house, but he couldn't help but notice a FedEx letter-size envelope from a sender whose name he recognized: Falcon Properties.

Falcon Properties was one of the largest developers of live-work-play communities in the country, and they had several developments throughout metro Atlanta. Nick's old condo, a unit in Decatur, had been part of their portfolio.

The FedEx package had been opened. He poured himself a serving of tea in a highball glass, and slipped the letter out of the envelope.

It was printed on heavy, expensive paper. It had a watermark, too.

As he read the correspondence, his heart began to boom.

This, he thought, *could be the answer to my problems.*

His mother entered the kitchen via the French doors. He looked up at her, waved the sheet of paper.

"Mom?" he asked. "Is this legit?"

"That? I was going to tell you about it today, actually. Yes, I think it's legitimate."

Nick licked his suddenly dry lips. He looked back at the page, but his gaze picked out only the key phrases.

Seeking to develop an upscale mixed-use community in the Macon, Georgia, area . . . your family's undeveloped woodlands property is a significant asset . . . we are prepared to tender a generous offer of approximately $5,000 per acre . . . could not reach your father so we are desiring to discuss with you . . .

"Did you talk to Grandpa Lee about this?" Nick asked.

"Come on, baby." Mom came to the counter, shook her head. "You know your granddaddy still doesn't have a telephone."

Nick wasn't surprised by that news. His Grandpa Lee was what the old heads in his family called "special."

Nick hadn't seen his maternal grandfather in over a decade. Grandpa Lee lived alone on that vast plot of undeveloped land outside of Macon, in a well-kept but modest residence. He had no phone; Nick believed he didn't have electricity, either, or plumbing.

He had a vehicle, Nick remembered, a Ford pickup truck, which at the time Nick had seen it was probably twenty-five years old. Grandpa Lee was most likely still driving it.

Occasionally, Grandpa Lee sent letters to Nick's mother, his only surviving child. His mother shared them with Nick. They were rambling missives in barely readable handwriting.

Despite his granddad's oddities, Nick had fond memories of spending time with him. Grandpa Lee had a sharp mind and a wicked sense of humor. There was no dispute that he was deeply attached to that property, too. On Nick's last visit, he had taken him on a tour of those woods—during daylight hours, as his granddad claimed, bizarrely, that it wasn't safe out there after dark—and Grandpa Lee had known the forest as well as a man knew his own den.

"But this, Mom, this is important," Nick said. He put the letter on the counter and placed his finger on it. "How many acres does Grandpa Lee have? I know it's a significant amount of land."

"It's about nine hundred acres." She watched him carefully.

Dizziness spun through Nick as he quickly did the math. "Mom, nine hundred acres, at five grand per acre, is *four point five million dollars.*"

"I can do mathematics, Nicholas." Arms crossed over her bosom, his mother stared at him as if he had sprouted a third eye in the center of his forehead. "That property has been in our family for generations, Nicholas. Do you think this is the first time we've had offers to sell it?" She uttered a harsh laugh. "Hell, we should count ourselves lucky that this time they offered payment for it instead of threatening to take it by force like they used to back in the day."

"I get it," Nick said. "Black folks never got the forty acres and a mule that was promised to us. We need to be property owners and pass down generational wealth, yada yada yada. But this is like a winning lottery ticket."

"You get it, huh?" Mom asked. "Are you sure about that?"

"The land is literally sitting there, vacant. Grandpa Lee's living in a tiny house—it's not as though he's got a commercial farm. Why not sell it? We could do so much with that money."

Mom had started to sip her tea, but instead put the glass on the counter and turned a penetrating stare on him.

"What's truly going on with you?" She gestured toward the letter. "I admit it's a fortune, but I'm quite comfortable in my retirement, and so is my dad, as odd as that may seem considering his living situation. I thought things were going well financially with you, too—heck, you've been living a life right out of that old TV show, *Lifestyles of the Rich and Famous*. What would they say— 'champagne wishes and caviar dreams.' Or am I missing something?"

"How often will an opportunity like this come along?" Nick asked, ignoring her question. "It's like selling a stock at the peak of a bull market. Six months from now, the real estate market could turn, and the land wouldn't be worth half as much."

"It wouldn't matter to your granddad if they offered him a hundred million dollars," Mom said. "And it wouldn't matter to him if they offered him a penny. It's not a financial decision. The property belongs to our family and must be passed down the line, no matter what. That's why he wouldn't talk to these people and they got in touch with me."

"You could make a deal with them?" Nick asked.

"Grandpa Lee holds the deed and he's presently of sound mind. No, I can't sign the deal, and I wouldn't if I could anyway. If any deal is to be made, your Grandpa Lee has to make it—and that's about as likely as a pig jumping over the moon."

"What if I go see him and talk to him about it?" Nick asked. "He might listen to me. This is ultimately my inheritance, too."

Mom laughed. "Child, you have no idea. But you know what— go ahead! Go see your grandpa and see how willing he is to listen to you about selling family property. You're long overdue to go see him anyway—heck, take Amiya, too. I think he'd like to meet her."

Still chuckling, Mom refreshed her iced tea and went back outside to the deck.

Nick lowered his head, drummed his fingertips on the countertop.

He wasn't prepared to let this go. He couldn't. It was his property, too—or would be, someday. Why didn't he have a vote in this situation?

His cell phone vibrated. It was a text message from Omar.

No payment plan . . . Shango says we got thirty days 2 pay in full . . . what we goin 2 do?

Nick used his iPhone to snap a photo of the letter. Fingers trembling, he sent a reply to Omar.

No worries . . . I have a plan.

6

That Saturday at six o'clock in the morning, Nick sat beside Amiya on his bed and gently shook her shoulder.

"Up and at 'em, beautiful," he said. "It's time to roll out."

Groaning, Amiya shifted away from him and snatched the sheets over her head.

"It's still dark," she said, her voice muffled.

"True, but I know you, girl. You take forever to get ready. We need to get to Grandpa Lee's place as early as we can."

Nick was already dressed in jeans and a polo shirt and had consumed his usual two cups of strong black coffee. He was not usually an early riser, but he'd been so charged with anticipation that he'd barely slept.

Earlier in the week, he had called Falcon Properties about the letter they had sent to his mother. A representative had confirmed the legitimacy of the offer and asked if the family was ready to proceed with an official contract, contingent upon an appraisal of the property. It had required every ounce of self-control in Nick for him to reply, "Not yet. We'll let you know soon."

But he'd already made plans for that money. Four and a half million dollars after federal and state taxes would be about 3.6 million. Grandpa Lee, who obviously had no interest in the financial windfall and drew a handsome pension from his Army service, could get a hundred thousand or so. The rest could be split between Nick and his mother, the sole living heirs to his grandfather's holdings.

With over 1.5 million dollars at his disposal, he could use a portion to pay off the gangster, Shango, and then he could sell his stake in Legacy Nutrition and do his own thing. He had decided that he couldn't stay in business with Omar and his shady associates. If they paid off Shango this one time, he would be back again in the future to shake them down, like a schoolyard bully demanding lunch money every day. The only way for Nick to avoid that outcome was for him to cut his ties and launch his own company, with his own money.

Nick hadn't disclosed any of his detailed plans with Amiya. He'd shared with her that he was going to discuss the matter of the property with Grandpa Lee, but little else. She disagreed with his intent; Amiya was too much like his mother in some ways, and bought into those rosy notions about generational wealth. He loved her, but he was a practical man, and he had to make plans for today.

"Hey." He shook Amiya again. "Come on, lady. We need to get going."

Amiya tossed off the sheets and sat up. She was nude, her typical manner of sleeping. Unable to resist, he reached for her leg, pulled her toward him, bent, and kissed the soft flesh of her upper thigh.

"I thought you wanted me to get dressed," she said. "But looks like you want to get freaky."

"Sorry." He smiled, rose from the bed. "Temporary lapse of judgment."

"Such a man." She pushed off the mattress and stretched her arms above her head. Even in the shadowed room, her body was a sight to behold.

She walked to the bathroom, and as she went past him he reached out to touch her butt. She playfully swatted his hand away.

"You said to get ready; now I'm getting ready," she said.

"Fine, fine," he said.

Forty-five minutes later, she was ready to go. As he'd advised her, she was casually dressed for a day in the country: floral print blouse, white gaucho pants, and comfortable flat-soled shoes. They loaded up in his Range Rover, and he pulled out of his garage into the early-morning sunshine.

"We can eat along the way," Nick said. "I can swing through a drive-thru, McDonald's or something like that."

"Are you serious?" Amiya puckered her lips. "Since when do I eat at McDonald's? Why can't we go somewhere decent and sit down?"

"It needs to be somewhere fast. We can't waste time having some long, leisurely breakfast."

They compromised on a local coffee shop and ate inside the restaurant, finding a table in the corner of the busy café. Amiya nibbled on a yogurt parfait, and Nick had ordered a sausage and egg sandwich.

"I'm struggling to understand the urgency to get to your grandfather's place." Amiya sipped her vanilla latte. "It's outside of Macon, correct? Only a two-hour drive?"

"A little less than that," Nick said. "But you have to understand, my grandfather is . . . different."

"Different how?"

"I already told you that he doesn't have a phone. Or electricity, or plumbing."

"So he lives off the grid." Amiya shrugged. "Nothing wrong with that. That's the new trend."

"You say that until you spend a little time there, and you realize how dependent we are on modern conveniences. When was the last time you had to use an outhouse?"

"Say no more." Amiya wrinkled her nose. "That's not mealtime conversation."

"But that's how he lives. He also has this weird thing about dusk, which is why I want to get there as early as we can. Grandpa Lee goes into total lockdown at sunset."

"Lockdown? What do you mean?"

"Just what I said, lockdown." Nick took a bite of his sandwich. "He won't let anyone stay in the house with him. He blows out the candles and lanterns. Then he takes out his shotgun and escorts you to your car and sees you off the property. No one stays there overnight, close family or not. Ironclad rule."

Amiya stared at him, her brown eyes huge with disbelief. After a beat, she blinked, broke into a grin.

"You're pulling my leg," she said.

"I wish I were. But I'm dead serious."

"What is he protecting himself against? Is there a problem with crime in the area?"

"Crime?" Nick laughed out loud. "He lives in the boondocks, babe. The backwoods. There's no crime there."

"There has to be an explanation, Nick. Wild animals?"

"Maybe." Nick shrugged. "Grandpa Lee won't discuss it. My mom doesn't have a clue either, but he's been like that for my entire life."

"I still think you're embellishing some things." Amiya swallowed a spoonful of her parfait. "I'm sure Grandpa Lee is only a sweet old man who decided he wants to live the simple life out in the country. He's probably a little skittish and set in his ways, but I'm sure he's fine."

"That's one way to look at it, I guess."

"He lives alone, correct?"

"For sure." Nick chuckled. "If my grandmother were still alive, I doubt she'd tolerate his eccentricities. There isn't that much love in the world."

"I put up with you." Amiya grinned.

Nick laughed. "Babe, there's no comparison. Grandpa's a veteran. He served in the Army for years, until he got wounded by shrapnel in some overseas conflict. He still gets around pretty well, though. Anyway, I always figured PTSD could explain why he acts the way he does at sunset. It's like he's hunkering down every night waiting for enemy soldiers to pass by."

"Possibly, but I'm going to do my best to resist psychoanalyzing him, no matter what you say," Amiya said. "I want to enjoy spending time with the eldest member of your mother's family, and soak up his wisdom. Anyone who's lived to the age of ninety has a slew of colorful stories and insights to share."

"He's got plenty of those." Nick checked his watch. "We'd better hit the road. We've got a long day ahead of us and we need to wrap it all up by sundown."

7

The driveway was so well-concealed in the lush spring foliage that Nick almost missed it.

He had been using the Google Maps app on his iPhone to navigate, supplementing the program with a set of handwritten directions from his mother, and still, he nearly missed the turn. They traveled on a narrow, twisting road lined on both sides with a nearly impenetrable growth of elms, maples, birch, and shrubs. The tree branches overhung the pavement, their boughs heavy with leaves, forming a canopy that cast the area into deep shadows and reminded Nick of driving through a cavern.

He had lowered his vehicle's speed to a crawl and was scanning the roadside for the mouth of the driveway when Amiya tapped his knee.

"There!" She pointed to the left.

He jabbed the brakes. Finally, he spotted the entrance to the property: a gravel lane almost completely hidden within the bushes. At the mouth of the driveway, a wrought-iron black mailbox stood on a weathered wooden post, festooned with white flowers. The name "L. Johnson" was painted on the mailbox in blocky white letters.

"You've got hawk eyes," he said. "I haven't been here in ten years and didn't remember what it looked like."

He turned onto the pathway, the SUV bouncing across the pavement. About fifteen feet beyond the road, a chain-link gate blocked access to the property. A sign hung on the middle of the barrier.

Private Property
No Trespassing!

"That's inviting," Amiya said. "I'm guessing your granddad doesn't like visitors dropping in? It looks like the gate has a padlock on it, too."

"We've got a key. Hang on a sec."

He got out and approached the gate. Pebbles and grit crunched underfoot. A cool, gentle breeze carried the fragrances of blooming flowers. It was a quarter past nine in the morning, and already the temperature had edged past eighty degrees, promising a sweltering day.

Other than his vehicle's humming engine, silence ruled the morning. The road that ran adjacent to his granddad's property entertained little traffic. Getting there, Nick had seen only a US postal mail truck, the driver weaving his way along the street.

He dug a ring of keys out of the front pocket of his jeans. Grandpa Lee had made copies for Nick's mother but no one else, and she had let Nick borrow them. He found a small key that looked as if it would fit, slipped it inside the locking mechanism, and disengaged the shackle.

He hung the lock on the chain link, and pulled the gate toward him, the metal swinging silently on oiled hinges.

Amiya had gotten behind the steering wheel. She guided the

Range Rover through the entrance. Once she'd driven past, Nick snapped the gate back into position.

He climbed onto the passenger side of the SUV. "You can drive on ahead. The house isn't too far."

Dense foliage crowded the driveway. Through the thick screen of interlocking vines, flowers, and shrubs, Nick saw immense pine, birch, and elm trees, and he wondered how long they had been standing. Although he had visited his reclusive grandfather many times, it was the first time he had questioned such things.

What would it look like back here once a developer stripped the land bare?

It wouldn't look nearly as bad as the fist of one of Shango's goons smashing into his jaw, would it?

"It's gorgeous back here," Amiya said as they rolled along the driveway. She had lowered her window, allowing the scents of the abundant flora to permeate the truck. "I can't imagine why you would possibly want your grandfather to sell this place."

"I can think of four and a half million reasons why."

"Money isn't everything, Nick."

"So says the woman whose family has a summer cottage on Martha's Vineyard."

"I know you love bringing up my family's money for some reason, but that's exactly why you should trust my opinion on this. Wealth doesn't bring happiness. My mom has lost more pairs of designer shoes than most people would ever buy in their lifetime and she's still absolutely miserable."

"At various points in my life, I've been both broke and flush with cash." He ran his fingers across the sleek dashboard and smiled. "I much prefer having cash."

"But look around. All of this land, hundreds of acres of it, this is a *legacy*. Do you want someone to rip all of these trees out of the earth and replace them with coffee shops and condos?"

"Give me the money and I don't care what they do with the trees. It's not my responsibility."

"You're wrong." Shaking her head, she sighed. "Clearly, we'll never agree on this."

"Since you haven't said yes to becoming Mrs. Alexander, we don't have to agree, do we?"

Her eyes burned like solar flares. He had gone too far, but the comment had slipped out of him, right past his psychological filter.

"That's how it's going to be, then?" she asked. "Because I'm still thinking about your proposal, you don't have to consider my opinion on things?"

"Amiya, on this topic of the property, let's agree to disagree, all right? You aren't changing my mind. Obviously, I'm not changing yours."

"Whatever you say." She wouldn't meet his gaze.

He would have to work his way back into her good graces. Amiya could carry a grudge for days, and his ill-considered remark had cut deep.

Still, her reluctance to move forward in their relationship bugged him. He didn't know what he had to prove to her to convince her to accept his ring.

But pissing her off like I just did isn't helping my case, he thought sourly.

At last, the land opened up, the narrow lane breaking off into several diverging branches that twisted through other areas of the property. One of those paths led to a small house. It was a shotgun-style residence; yellow with green trim, and from the looks of it, had been recently painted.

"Wow, is this the house?" Amiya asked.

"Grandpa Lee's mansion." Nick chuckled.

A blue Ford pickup truck so old that it looked as if it belonged in an automobile museum was parked underneath a wooden carport.

Nick grinned. "He's driving the same truck, too. Thing's gotta be thirty-something years old. Looks like it's in great condition, though."

A garden thrived near the house. It was about the size of a regulation basketball court, enclosed within a waist-high fence.

A squat, mahogany-skinned man shuffled through the middle of the garden. He wore denim overalls and a khaki bucket cap hat. He was intent on his work, head bowed, a shovel balanced like a rifle over his shoulder.

"Grandpa's in the garden." Nick pointed. Giddiness flitted through him; he felt like a kid again, a reaction he hadn't expected. "Let's park and go see him."

8

Amiya parked underneath the carport beside Grandpa Lee's old pickup, and they hopped out of the SUV. Nick reached for Amiya's hand as they walked across the front yard toward the garden. A cloud passed across her eyes. He figured she wasn't going to forgive him so easily for his Mrs. Alexander comment.

"Can we try to enjoy this visit?" he asked.

With obvious reluctance, she allowed him to take her hand. He lifted her fingers to his lips, kissed them.

"Don't forget, you're in the penalty box," she said.

"I'll make it up to you before the day's over."

They walked past Grandpa Lee's house. Up close, Nick saw that it was in almost perfect condition, as if it had been restored by a crack team of contractors. A bench-style swing rocked on the veranda, hanging from a pair of glistening silver chains. The front door, painted a deep shade of red, seemed to shimmer. Sunshine sparkled on the windows, and potted plants lined the porch railing.

From what Nick remembered, Grandpa Lee had always done his own maintenance and repairs, on both his vehicle and his property.

He didn't share his grandfather's talents; changing a light bulb was the limit of his handyman skills.

They approached the garden. White butterflies fluttered around his grandfather, like a halo of fairies. Grandpa Lee suddenly swung away from his labors and spotted them. He pushed up his glasses on his nose. His lips broke into a broad grin.

He looks damned good, Nick thought, *to be ninety years old.* Grandpa Lee's thick beard was snow-white, but vitality glistened in his eyes.

"There he is!" Grandpa Lee said. He stepped toward them through a row of string beans, slightly favoring his left leg, and came through the garden's open gate.

"Hey, Grandpa Lee," Nick said. "It's so good to see you again."

He extended his arm to shake his grandfather's hand, but Grandpa Lee shoved his hand aside and pulled him into a bear hug. His grandfather smelled faintly of perspiration, but mostly of rich, raw earth, as if he had recently been formed from red Georgia clay.

Nick was probably three inches taller than his grandfather, placing his elder at about five-feet-seven, but Grandpa Lee had the wide-shouldered build of a powerlifter, and the embrace of one, too. He squeezed Nick so fiercely that Nick struggled to breathe.

"You've been on my heart lately, son," Grandpa Lee said in his ear. "It's a blessing that you came down today."

"It's been too long," Nick said, and meant it.

"Who's this here?" Grandpa Lee let him go and smiled at Amiya. "Is this fine lady here your wife? I never got an invitation to a wedding, son."

"This is my girlfriend, Amiya," Nick said. He slid his gaze toward Amiya. "I'm still working on the wife part."

Amiya ignored Nick, smiled at his grandfather. "I'm pleased to meet you, sir."

"You better work harder, son!" Grandpa Lee laughed. He peeled off his work gloves, gently took one of Amiya's hands, and bowed. "Welcome to Westbrook, young lady. The pleasure's all mine."

"Westbrook?" Amiya asked, her gaze flitting from Grandpa Lee to Nick.

"I had forgotten all about that name," Nick said. "Westbrook—it's just what Grandpa calls the property here."

"It's not just what I call it," Grandpa Lee said. "It's the proper name of the land, passed down through generations of our family."

Here we go, Nick thought, and shot Amiya a look.

"It's lovely here." She clasped her hands together and turned that killer smile of hers on Grandpa Lee. "Would you mind taking us on a tour?"

9

For Amiya, touring Grandpa Lee's property was like going back in time.

Grandpa Lee—he insisted that he call her by that name, as if she were already a member of the family—kicked off the tour by taking them inside his house. It was a true shotgun house, so named because shooting a gun through the front door would carry the buckshot all the way through to the back: the residence had only two rooms, with no door, wall, or partition separating them. The front room contained a double bed in a weathered oak frame, a tall bookcase packed with hardcover volumes, and an oak writing desk with a Mason jar full of pencils, a folded newspaper lying in the center. A kerosene lantern stood on a small table beside the bed.

A stacked-stone fireplace dominated the wall opposite the bed. Cords of firewood were stacked in a neat pile in a wire bin.

The back room had a wood-burning stove fashioned from cast iron. A kitchen table with another kerosene lamp, and four wooden chairs gathered around the table. A big wash basin stood in a corner.

Nick had warned her that his grandfather eschewed modern

conveniences but seeing it in the flesh amazed Amiya. It was as if she were on a tour of a historic home from the early nineteenth century.

The floors, comprised exclusively of hickory hardwood, glistened underneath her feet. The interior of the entire place was immaculate. Amiya had grown up in a spacious home where regular maid service was commonplace, but the cleanliness of Grandpa Lee's house far surpassed her experience.

"This is amazing," Amiya said. "Can I take a photo?"

Grandpa Lee smiled, shrugged. Amiya asked him and Nick to pose together in front of the stove. She snapped the picture, checked it, found it looked good, and then frowned.

"I don't have mobile service," she said to Nick.

"Welcome to the backwoods, baby." Nick slipped out his iPhone. "I don't have service, either. No surprise."

Uneasiness tightened her stomach. She glanced at Grandpa Lee. "Is that common, out here?"

"I couldn't tell you, young lady. I don't have one of those gadgets. Ain't got no need for any of that mess."

"But, living here, do you ever miss television?" she asked. "Or the internet?"

"I've got plenty of books." He indicated the bookcase with a sweep of his arm. "I get the local newspaper delivered each day. What else do I need for entertainment and information?"

"No distractions, right, Grandpa?" Nick said.

"No landline telephone, either?" Amiya looked around.

"That's what the mail is for, isn't it? Anyone who wants to contact me can send me a letter, like my grandson here did, telling me y'all were coming for a visit today."

"But what would you do in case of an emergency?" Amiya asked. She was genuinely concerned about his safety. Grandpa Lee appeared to be in good health, but he was ninety years old and lived alone, miles away from civilization.

"If it's my time, then it's my time." Grandpa Lee shrugged.

Amiya glanced at Nick, and he shrugged, too—his movements

almost eerily like his grandfather's. In the short time that she had watched the two men together, she had picked up on little nuances they shared: the way they shrugged their shoulders, how they put their fists on their waists, their facial expressions when they laughed. They were fifty years apart in age but more alike than she could have imagined.

Will Nick also someday tire of modern living and decide he wants to live totally off the grid like his grandfather? Amiya wondered. What was in the future for Nick—and how did she fit in it?

She knew Nick was eager to marry her, but she had concerns about his reasons for wanting them to walk down the aisle together. She felt as if she merely matched some predefined list that he had created—her physical attributes, education, career path, and family background—and that his desire was less about who she really was as an individual, and was more about his *idea* of her. She had grown to love him, but she couldn't commit to a future together until she believed he truly saw her, and loved her, and not some romanticized ideal.

She'd wanted to learn more about his family, too, which was partly why she had anticipated this trip to meet his grandfather. From her studies in psychology, she had learned that the past often repeated itself, in cycles, throughout generations. Learning about Grandpa Lee would grant her more insights about Nick.

Her suspicion so far was that Nick didn't want his grandfather to sell the land. He seemed proud of how his granddad lived, of what he had accomplished living off the land using his bare hands and his intellect. She was increasingly convinced that external factors were driving Nick's intent. Perhaps business troubles or debts, or some soaring ambition to go into a capital-intensive enterprise. She hadn't pushed for an answer.

Eventually, the truth would reveal itself.

"Let's keep on moving, y'all." Grandpa Lee opened the door at the back of the house.

Amiya filed outside. A green shed-like structure stood about twenty feet away from the back door. Her stomach curdled.

"The outhouse?" she asked.

Grandpa Lee grinned. "Uh-huh. You need to use it?"

"Grandpa, she made me stop, *twice*, on the way here so she could use the ladies' room," Nick said. "She has no intention of going in there."

"You're one hundred percent correct," Amiya said.

"But I keep it clean." Grandpa Lee ambled to the building and swung open the door. Inside, she saw a gleaming wood commode, the lid closed.

"It's a compost toilet, young lady," he said. "I installed it a couple years back. It doesn't stink one bit."

Amiya advanced a few steps closer. She detected no foul odors. She caught the fragrance of a pine-scented disinfectant, actually, and noticed a plastic spray bottle hanging from a hook on the wall.

"That bowl's so clean, you could eat off it," Grandpa Lee said.

"No doubt, but I'll pass," Amiya said.

Grandpa Lee cackled and motioned for them to follow.

He pointed out the entrance to his storm cellar, located about thirty feet away from the house. A locked pair of heavy oak doors secured the underground chamber. Down there, he explained, he kept provisions such as canned goods, bags of rice, flour, and sugar, and other items.

Next, he pointed out the water well, located not far from the cellar. Amiya was about to voice a concern about a ninety-year-old man lifting heavy buckets of water and carrying them across the property, and thought better of it. Who was she to judge? Perhaps such physically demanding labors had contributed toward Grandpa Lee's good health.

Farther away, he showed them another shed-like building that Amiya first thought was another outhouse, but was actually a smokehouse.

"I get my meats from the market in town," Grandpa Lee said. He nodded toward the forested land beyond. "But the fish I catch from the lake here. Have you ever been fishing, sweetheart?"

"Once, when I was a child," Amiya said.

"We'll have to do that here sometime," Grandpa Lee said.

"I'm surprised that you've got a lake on the property," Amiya said. "Nick didn't say anything about that to me."

"Sorry," Nick said. "I didn't remember. I haven't been here in ten years."

"Let's take a drive." Grandpa Lee clapped Nick on the shoulder. "I'll show y'all what we've got out there."

10

The three of them piled into Grandpa Lee's pickup truck. Grandpa Lee got behind the wheel, Amiya sat in the middle, and Nick squeezed into the final spot and slammed the door shut behind him.

Nick was waiting for the right moment to bring up selling the property. He had no idea how Grandpa Lee would respond, but his grandfather seemed to be in high spirits, eager to share his world with them, and Nick didn't want to disrupt the mood, not just yet.

But the offer letter felt as if it were burning a hole in his back pocket.

He noticed that the Ford's interior, like his granddad's house, was spotless. It smelled richly of leather and a pleasant, pine-scented air freshener. The dashboard gleamed.

"What year is this truck?" Nick asked.

"It's a 1982 Ford F-150," Grandpa Lee said. "I've got a hundred and ten thousand miles on the odometer, but I bet I could outlast your high-end vehicle right there." He snickered.

The engine started with a throaty rumble. The truck was a stick shift—Nick remembered that his grandfather had actually taught him how to drive a stick—and Grandpa Lee shifted gears easily into reverse. If Nick had checked under the hood he knew he would have found that the engine was as well maintained as the interior. His granddad was one of those rare guys who knew how to repair damn near anything.

"The rifle mounted on the rear windshield," Amiya said, turning slightly to glance behind her. "Why do you need that?"

"That's a Remington 700 rifle," Grandpa Lee said. "I'm a country boy at heart. I keep a gun in my truck and one on my hip; always have."

"You've never needed to use it?" Amiya asked. "I was thinking you might have deer or other critters on the property that you needed to regulate."

"If I ever needed to use my gun here at Westbrook, we've got bigger problems," Grandpa Lee said.

Grandpa Lee steered the truck away from the house and onto one of the narrow dirt lanes that snaked deep into the woods beyond. They bounced along the path.

"Nick told me about how you lock down the house at night," Amiya said. "What's that all about?"

"Is this a therapy session?" Nick asked. "Come on, babe."

She shot him a look. "I don't mean to be rude. I was only curious. Grandpa Lee is a grown man and can speak for himself."

Grunting, Grandpa Lee glanced at his watch, squinted at the sky. "We've about ten hours of daylight left. That's a good bit of time for us to enjoy Westbrook and get you kids on your way back home before dusk."

"What happens here at dusk?" Amiya asked, and Nick wanted to sink onto the floor.

"It's better to be in the house," Grandpa Lee said.

"But why?" she asked. "It seems nighttime out here would be gorgeous—there's no city lights or buildings to block the view of the stars. I'm only trying to understand this in-by-dark rule."

"Some things you don't need to understand," Grandpa Lee said, in a tone that suggested the matter was closed for further discussion.

Thankfully, Amiya let it go. She could be like a bulldog sometimes, a quality that Nick often appreciated about her, but this was one of those instances when it would have been simply rude to keep up the questioning. They were guests of their grandfather, and he was taking time out of his day to show them around—pissing him off wouldn't have gained them anything. Especially considering the potentially explosive discussion Nick planned to broach later on.

Nevertheless, like Amiya, he *did* wonder about Grandpa Lee's unreasonable fear of sunset. What, exactly, was he afraid of? Nick's best guess was that there might have been bears or something roaming the property. But if that were true, why couldn't Grandpa Lee just say so? Why was he so cryptic about his reasons?

They drove on in silence for several minutes. The surrounding foliage crowded the dirt track, but came short of rendering it impassable. Nick could envision his meticulous grandfather out here with a pair of hedge shears, clipping away the invasive undergrowth.

"We're crossing over the creek up here," Grandpa Lee said. "When we go over that bridge, we're in Westbrook proper."

Amiya glanced at Nick, a question in her eyes. Nick offered only a shrug. He didn't understand what his grandfather meant about "Westbrook proper," didn't understand why he had given the place a name when it didn't appear as such on any official map of the area. Grandpa Lee had his eccentric ways.

The bridge spanned about fifteen feet, arching over a bubbling creek. Fashioned from hardwood, the narrow bridge was in excellent condition and held steady as Grandpa Lee steered the truck across.

A wave of heat passed over Nick as they crossed over the creek. Next to him, he felt Amiya tense, too. Then the odd sensation subsided.

Weird, Nate thought. Perhaps it had been only a warm draft of air blowing through the truck's open windows; the morning was already getting hotter.

"Did you construct that bridge, too?" Amiya asked.

"My granddaddy built it," he said. "I've only had to maintain it."

"It's amazing that your family has held onto this land for so long," Amiya said. "Passing it down from one generation to the next. It's admirable."

Nick nudged Amiya with his elbow. *Knock it off.*

"I'm sure Nick looks forward to inheriting Westbrook someday," Amiya said.

Nick had to bite his tongue to prevent himself from cussing. He could not believe she was gleefully sabotaging his entire reason for coming here.

"We'll get around to talking about that when the time is right," Grandpa Lee said.

"Yes, we will," Nick said. He stared at Amiya as he said: "It's private, *family* business."

But Amiya only smiled at him and rubbed his knee. He was beginning to regret that he had invited her to come with him, and couldn't wait to get her alone so he could blast her.

The truck bounced along on the dirt path, winding deeper into the woods. It might have been only Nick's imagination, but to him it seemed that once they crossed over the bridge, the forest got thicker: the trees seemed taller, the flowers more vibrant, the smells wafting through the open windows more aromatic.

The wildlife was more abundant, too. He spotted fat squirrels scampering along tree boughs. Birds wheeling high above in the crowns of the trees. What looked like a doe stood off near some shrubs about a dozen yards away, the animal watching them rumble past.

What would happen if the real estate developer took over this property? Nick thought. *Would they send in a team of hunters to exterminate the deer and the other animals?*

He couldn't worry about it. Such things were the price of progress, and happened every day.

"It's lovely back here," Amiya said.

"Wait until you see the lake," Grandpa Lee said. He drove around a bend in the road and brought the truck to a stop next to a pine tree. "Here we go. We've gotta walk from here."

They climbed out of the pickup, shut the doors. Standing outside of the vehicle, the sheer immensity of these woods washed over Nick. Although his mother had said that they owned nine hundred acres, the forest felt much bigger than that, and seemed far more isolated than its physical location could logically explain. He didn't hear any aircraft buzzing past overhead, couldn't detect any distant sounds of vehicles. The primacy of undisturbed nature pressed on him like a tangible weight.

I'm just a city slicker, out of my element, Nick thought.

He glanced at Amiya. She had a wide-eyed expression as she looked around, and he supposed she shared his thoughts.

"Come on, y'all," Grandpa Lee said.

Hands shoved in his overall pockets, Grandpa Lee picked his way ahead on a worn dirt path that twisted through the trees. Amiya followed behind him, and Nick brought up the rear.

Nick noted the density of the tree canopy; leaves obstructed most of the morning's sunshine, casting the land around them into deep shadow. Amiya looked over her shoulder at where Grandpa Lee had parked the truck. Concern wrinkled her face.

"It seems like you could easily get lost out here," she said.

"If you don't know where you're going," Nick said. "I definitely wouldn't want to get caught out here at night."

"Just on ahead, kids," Grandpa Lee said.

A few minutes later, they broke through the woods and came into a clearing. They had reached the shore of the lake. The lake itself, shimmering in the sunlight, spread across an area of several acres. Gulls swooped and dipped to skim the surface. Perhaps a dozen yards away, Nick saw a gaggle of geese wading into the water.

"Welcome to Westbrook Lake," Grandpa Lee said. He ambled to a nearby tree stump and eased down onto it. He snatched a handkerchief out of his front pocket, pulled off his bucket cap hat, and mopped sweat off his bald head and face.

"This is beautiful," Amiya said, hands on her hips as she swept her gaze back and forth. She glanced at Nick. "You used to come here as a kid?"

"During summers, yeah," he said. "Grandpa would bring me here to fish."

"Still plenty of fish in there, son," Grandpa Lee said. He pulled his hat snug on his head again. "Should have brought your rod and reel. We can do that next time you come through—don't wait ten years 'til your next visit." He chuckled.

"Walk with me," Amiya said, and grasped Nick's fingers.

Hand in hand, they strolled along the grassy shore. Nick looked over his shoulder. Grandpa Lee stayed behind on the stump, gazing out at the water, immersed in private thoughts.

After they had walked a bit, Amiya turned around. She positioned Nick's hands along the rise of her hips, slipped her arms around his neck, and pulled him forward into a soft, lingering kiss.

"This must mean you've forgiven me for my earlier transgression," Nick said when their lips parted.

"Maybe." She kissed him again, pressed her pelvis against his, and his body responded in kind. "It's so gorgeous out here, it makes me feel . . ."

"Horny?" He grinned.

"Liberated." She gestured toward the water. "Think about it. This lake, this land, has been here, untouched, for over a hundred years. It's pristine."

"Not quite pristine," Nick said, and nodded at a spot behind her. "Check that out."

About twenty feet away, in the mud at the edge of the lake, lay the eviscerated corpse of an animal about the size of a small dog. A dark haze of flies buzzed around the creature.

"What the heck is that?" Amiya wrinkled her nose.

"I think it's a river otter. I don't know what got ahold of it. A bear maybe?"

"There are bears out here?" She nervously scanned the shoreline and the woods beyond.

"I've never seen one, but probably. It could have been a coyote, too. We've got those in these parts."

"Next thing you'll be telling me that there are lions and tigers out here, too." She took his hand. "Little wonder Grandpa Lee keeps a handgun and a rifle. Let's get back."

"Y'all kids have fun over there?" Grandpa Lee asked. "Thought I was gonna have to fetch you some hay to roll in."

Amiya blushed, but Nick only smiled. "You know how it is, Grandpa."

"Don't I remember." Grandpa Lee squinted as he looked at the rippling waters. "Good ole days. How times have changed."

"Yeah, about that," Nick said. His heart knocked. He retrieved the copy of the letter from his back pocket and unfolded it.

"Nick," Amiya said, voice strained. "Is this an appropriate time for that?"

Nick ignored her, but his hands shook as he straightened out the paper. Grandpa Lee looked from Amiya to Nick. His brow furrowed.

"What is it?" Grandpa Lee asked.

"Mom got a letter in the mail earlier this week," Nick said. He cleared his throat. "It's from Falcon Properties. They contacted Mom because they couldn't get in touch with you."

"I get those letters from those property companies, I throw 'em in the trash, don't open 'em," Grandpa Lee said. He spat on the ground. "They don't have anything I want."

"You should look at this one," Nick said. He offered the letter to his grandfather.

Grandpa Lee stared at the paper in Nick's hand.

"They're offering five thousand dollars an acre, Grandpa," Nick said. "With all the land we've got back here, that's a sum of over four and a half million dollars. A fortune. We should take the offer."

"Sell . . . sell Westbrook?" Grandpa spoke slowly, as if the words belonged to a foreign tongue.

"Nick, please," Amiya said.

Nick silenced her with a sharp look, turned back to his grandfather.

"We may never get an offer like this again," Nick said. "We need to take it. I can give them a call on Monday and tell them to draw up the contract."

Slowly, Grandpa Lee rose from the tree stump. With a grunt, he snatched the letter out of Nick's fingers.

He began to tear it to pieces.

"Hey, come on, man," Nick said.

"Not selling, goddammit . . ." Grandpa Lee said. He lowered his head, gasped. A violent cough shook him. Redness sprayed from his lips and spattered against the half-shredded letter in his hands.

Is that blood? Nick thought. *Oh, Jesus.*

Coughing explosively, his body wracked by the savage force of each spasm, Grandpa Lee sank to his knees in the dirt. His eyes rolled back, exposing the whites. Scraps of torn paper, dotted with blood, spun from his hands and scattered across the earth.

Nick rushed forward, Amiya right behind him. He got his arms around his granddad before he could hit the ground, and Amiya helped support him, too.

Grandpa Lee was heavier than he looked, like a dead weight in his embrace. He sagged against Nick. His bifocals hung askew on his face. A frothy mixture of blood and saliva bubbled on his lips.

Nick was dizzy from the sudden turn of events, paralyzed by indecision. He'd never seen anyone collapse like that, had no idea what to do.

Grandpa Lee's eyes had slid shut.

"He's still breathing," Amiya said, perspiration beading her brow. She clasped Grandpa Lee's hand in hers. "He's got a pulse, he's still with us. We've gotta get him help, right now, or . . ."

Amiya left the sentence unfinished, but even in the stupefied daze that had slipped over him, Nick realized what she had been about to say.

Or he's going to die.

11

Nick fumbled with his cell phone but couldn't get a signal. Amiya tried hers and couldn't get service, either.

"It didn't work back at the house," Nick said. "It damn sure isn't working out here in the sticks. Shit."

"Okay, let's think, then." Amiya sucked in her bottom lip. "All right. We get him to the hospital ourselves. One can't be too far. Macon's about ten miles away, correct?"

"Something like that." Nick looked at Grandpa Lee in his arms. His chest rose and fell slowly, but he appeared comatose. Nick found the handkerchief in his granddad's front pocket and used it to wipe away the bloody saliva pasted across his lips. He felt a slow but steady pulse in his granddad's throat.

Please don't die on me, Grandpa, Nick thought, his chest tight with emotion. *Please.*

"He's going to be okay." Amiya touched Nick's shoulder, squeezed. "He's a tough man."

Nick blinked away the hot tears that hung in his eyes, nodded at her.

"Help me carry him," he said. "I'll get my hands under his arms, and you can grab his feet."

"Let's do it."

He hooked his hands in Grandpa Lee's armpits and Amiya lifted up his legs by grasping his leather boots at the ankles. Nick looked over his shoulder and located the narrow dirt trail they had traveled through the woods to get to the lake.

"You lead," he said to Amiya. "We'll follow that trail back to the truck."

Amiya nodded tightly, and they started off. Earlier, it had taken about ten minutes to walk to the lake, and this time, with an incapacitated Grandpa Lee in tow, their progress was significantly slower. They bumped against trees. Shrubs scraped across their arms and face. Insects buzzed past. More than once, they almost dropped his grandfather, but somehow maintained a hold on him.

As they dragged him along, Nick's mind doubled back to what had happened—Grandpa Lee snatching that letter out of his hand; blood spraying from his lips and spattering the page—and he could not escape the idea that all of this was his fault, that his pushing his grandfather to sell the land had upset him so much that it had triggered a health crisis. A sense of guilt pressed on him, as tangible as the heat waves permeating the woods.

Please, Grandpa Lee, hold on, he thought.

When Nick finally spotted the truck through the trees, he wanted to scream with relief. His arms ached and he was drenched in sweat. Amiya, too, looked as if she had endured a brutal workout, her hair frizzy and perspiration glistening on her cheeks.

They emerged from the thicket and dragged Grandpa Lee to the pickup truck.

"All right," Nick said, panting. "We get him in the front seat now. You hold him and I'll drive."

Amiya swung open the passenger door and climbed onto the bench seat. Nick maneuvered around, his hands still hooked under Grandpa Lee's arms. Together, he and Amiya heaved Grandpa Lee up and into the truck, another strenuous effort. Nick raced around the front of the pickup and hustled behind the wheel.

Grandpa Lee had left the key in the ignition. The engine kicked on with a low rumble.

"You remember the way back?" Amiya asked. She was pressed against Nick, her arms gathered around Grandpa Lee's torso.

"Yeah, I used to come out here with him all the time."

But the reality was that in his frazzled state, he wasn't sure of the route back to the house. On the way there to the lake, his granddad had made several turns, branching from one narrow dirt lane to the next without the benefit of directional signs or markers of any kind that Nick had seen. It would have done no good to share that news with Amiya. The land covered nine hundred acres and they had a truck—they would find their way back.

The question was whether it would be soon enough for Grandpa Lee.

Nick worked the manual gear shift. The gears protested with a grating whine.

"Do you know how to drive a stick?" Amiya asked.

"It's been years, but I know how." He gritted his teeth, wiped a drop of salty sweat out of the corner of his eye. "Relax and let me focus."

She mumbled something under her breath, but he couldn't be concerned about her opinions. All that mattered was getting medical attention for his grandfather.

He shifted into reverse and popped the clutch. The truck jerked backward, tossing them forward, and Amiya let out a thin cry of surprise.

"Sorry," he said. "I've got it now."

Amiya gathered her bearings, adjusted her hold on Grandpa Lee. Nick backed up in a half-circle and pointed the Ford in the direction from which they had originally come. He shifted again, working the pedals. The truck leaped forward.

"Hang on, guys," Nick said as the pickup plowed ahead. The

speedometer inched up to thirty miles per hour, the maximum speed that Nick felt comfortable reaching on such a narrow, unpredictable road. Foliage breezed past. The tree canopy disappeared in sections, allowing spears of sunlight to penetrate the woods.

They neared an intersection. Nick went with his first instinct and hung a right.

"I thought we should have made a left there," Amiya said.

"You've never visited before." He increased their speed back up to thirty. "How's he doing?"

"His pulse is slow but steady. He's hanging on."

"We'll be out of here in a few minutes."

They approached another juncture of diverging paths. Nick hesitated only a second and made a left.

"I don't remember coming this way," Amiya said.

"How would you? Everything looks the same—foliage and trees. Let me drive, okay?"

Amiya quieted. But apprehension had begun to spread like heartburn through his gut. *It's only nine hundred acres*, he reminded himself. *We'll get out of here soon enough.* He shifted into a higher gear, pouring on the speed. The speedometer tipped toward forty miles an hour.

"You're going too fast, Nick."

"Damn, girl, will you knock it off—"

Something big and fast raced across the path ahead of them, dangerously close. Amiya screamed. Nick cursed and twisted the wheel to avoid hitting the animal. The truck swerved to the left and bounced off the dirt path. Frantic, Nick pumped the brakes, but it was too late: they slammed head-on into a massive tree.

The impact flung him forward, and all he knew was darkness.

12

Someone was shaking Nick's shoulder, and a voice spoke to him, so muted it was as if he were hearing it while floating deep in a cold, black sea.

"Nick . . . grandfather . . . gone . . ."

Nick opened his eyes. The warm, salty taste of blood filled his mouth. Pain sizzled across his head.

Hit something, he thought. *Wasn't wearing a seat belt.*

He blinked, winced from the throbbing headache. The world spun with shadows and smoke, and slowly his vision cleared. He was in the pickup truck on the side of the road, the front end jammed against a pine tree. Gray tendrils of smoke twisted from underneath the hood. The engine knocked and sputtered.

"Nick." Amiya clutched his shoulder. "Grandpa Lee. He's gone."

Nick turned. Amiya's curly bangs hung in her face, and he saw a comma of blood on the side of her mouth. An ugly bruise was forming above her right eye.

She wasn't wearing a seat belt, either, he thought.

But the meaning of her words finally sank in.

"Gone?" he asked. The taste of blood filled his mouth, and he spat. "He's . . . he's dead?"

She sniffled, shook her head. "I don't know . . . he's not here. I blacked out like you did and when I woke up, I saw my door open. He's gone."

"He got out of the truck on his own? How? He was . . . he was unconscious."

"I don't know." Tears streamed from her eyes.

"We've gotta find him." Nick switched off the ignition, concerned by the sputters and the smoke. He went to open his door. Dizziness sloshed through him. He sucked in a couple of deep, stabilizing breaths.

He tried to get out again, but discovered his side of the truck was sunken against a thick growth of shrubs that obstructed the door. Amiya scrambled out on the passenger side. He followed her.

Dropping to the thick, tall grass outside the pickup, he had to seize the door handle to keep from losing his balance. He pulled in a jagged breath. It felt as if someone had slugged him in the chest, and he figured the steering wheel had smashed against his sternum when he had crashed.

Amiya had wandered onto the dirt lane. Using her hand as a visor against the sun's glare, she looked around.

"I don't see him," she said.

"He's got to be close by," Nick said. He shouted: "Grandpa Lee! Can you hear us? Grandpa Lee!"

"Grandpa Lee!" Amiya called.

In answer, he heard only the breeze flapping through the woods, and the annoyingly cheerful chirping of birds.

Nick could not stomach the idea that his granddad, in the midst of a medical crisis, had slipped out of the truck and was staggering through the forest, weak and incoherent. The possibility struck him with a nearly paralyzing anguish.

"Let's search the immediate area," Nick said. "We weren't unconscious for long. He can't have gone far."

"You think he's walking home?" she asked.

"How the hell would I know?"

From the surprised look of hurt on Amiya's face, he realized he had yelled. He pushed out a breath, touched her arm.

"Sorry," he said. "Let's do our best to find him, okay? Look for any sign of him. I'll search on this side of the road, and you take the other side."

"Okay," she said. "Don't wander too far away. Keep the truck in sight. We can't lose each other."

They searched for several minutes, both of them calling Grandpa Lee's name. Nick expected to find his grandfather sprawled face down on the ground somewhere in the woods, unconscious or worse. He didn't know how he would respond to finding his grandpa in that condition; he didn't know if he could handle it. Already, he was wrestling with a growing sense of guilt that accumulated like bile in his throat.

His search turned up nothing. He wandered back to the truck. Amiya emerged from the trees on the other side of the lane about a minute later. She had leaves in her hair, but her eyes told him everything.

"It doesn't make any sense," Nick said. "But he must be farther away than we thought."

"But is he alert? Does he know where he's headed? Or is he in a confused state of mind?"

"If he were thinking logically, he wouldn't have left us," Nick said.

"I still can't get a signal." Amiya had slipped out her cell phone again, swiped her thumb across the display.

"We won't. Forget about the phones."

Sighing, Amiya jammed her phone back into her small purse. "We need to get back to the house. I'm thinking Grandpa Lee, even in an agitated state of consciousness, would be drawn back home."

"Right. We need to find our way there."

"Find our way there?" She stared at him. "You said you knew your way around out here, Nick. Do you recognize where we are?"

"Well . . ." Nick looked away from her. A nervous laugh slipped out of him.

"What's funny?" she asked.

"Honest?" He met her gaze. "Babe, I have no idea where we are. I don't recognize any of this."

"But back at the lake, you said you used to come out here all the time and you knew the way home." Her eyes sharpened into tiny darts. "Was that the truth?"

"I thought I knew the way back, okay? But I wasn't exactly thinking clearly after I saw my granddad coughing up blood and passing out in my arms. Can you give me a break here?"

Lips tightening into a firm line, Amiya turned away from him. She put her hands against the side of the pickup, lowered her head, breathing deeply.

"It's nine hundred acres," he said. "To put it into perspective: that's about a mile and a half of square mileage, like a small town. It's not as though we're lost in the middle of some vast Alaskan wilderness. We'll find our way back."

"I'm driving this time." Amiya flung open the passenger door and got inside.

Nick shrugged, climbed in after her.

She twisted the key in the ignition. The engine sputtered, but didn't catch.

"It's damaged from the collision," Nick said. "I don't know for sure what ran across the road. I think it was a deer—if so it's probably better that we smacked the tree."

"Regardless, it's not helping us now." She switched off the ignition, and switched it on again, pumping the gas pedal. The truck coughed but the engine wouldn't turn over. Amiya cursed and tried it again, but it was no use.

"We can walk," Nick said. "Maybe it's better to walk, maybe we can keep a closer eye out for my granddad."

At the mention of his grandfather, the anger seemed to seep out of her. She slid the key out of the ignition and placed it in her purse. Flicking hair out of her eyes, she looked at him.

"Before we go, let's see what's in the truck that we can take with us," she said.

13

Amiya was pissed.

What had begun as a perfectly charming jaunt in the country, complete with a tour of a fully operational rustic home, had devolved into some off-the-beaten-path nightmare. Grandpa Lee was sick, possibly dying, and wandering alone through the woods. She had been in a vehicle accident and was shaken up. To top it off, she was stuck with Nick, who was responsible for their entire predicament and had no clue how to return to the house.

If they didn't have a pressing need to get moving, she would have cussed him out, and she wasn't one to use foul language. She had grown up in a chaotic house with a domineering mother who often exploded into screaming fits over even trivial matters, and she had determined that she wouldn't follow in her mom's footsteps. She strived to avoid drama.

Still, she was angry. But she channeled that emotion toward action.

When she suggested doing an inventory of the items in the truck, Nick, predictably, demurred.

"Is it really necessary to go through all of this stuff?" He stood beside the pickup, hands on his waist. "We'll be at the house within half an hour."

"I want to take the rifle." She climbed over the truck's rear lift gate and onto the flatbed. The bottom was so clean it gleamed in the sunshine, the metal simmering underneath her flats.

The Remington 700 was secured within a metal rack bolted at the edge of the rear windshield. Carefully, she lifted it out. The rifle was warm in her hands.

"You don't know how to use a gun," Nick said.

Amiya checked the chamber and found it was already loaded. She positioned the nylon strap across her shoulders, the rifle hanging across her back.

Nick stared at her, lips parted in surprise.

"Why are you shocked?" she asked. "Please, get up here and help me look through this tool box."

"When did you learn about guns?" He clambered onto the flatbed.

"I did have a life before you came along. One of my brothers is a firearms enthusiast. He taught me some things, took me to firing ranges."

Distantly, thunder rumbled. Amiya looked to the sky and noticed that dark storm clouds were forming into a thick tapestry.

"I still don't think this is necessary." Nick stood beside her on the truck. "We could already be on our way back, or could have found my granddad."

"I want to be prepared for anything. Nothing today has gone according to plan."

"Right." Nick winced as if poked with a hot iron. "You think all of this is my fault?"

"I didn't say that." She snapped open the latches of the aluminum Kobalt tool box bolted to the front of the flatbed. "But it is what it is."

"My fault then, huh? Everything is on me."

"You seem determined to pin the blame on yourself. Guess what?

If the shoe fits, wear it. I don't have the inclination to join your little pity party."

She heard him suck in a breath, and she thought he was going to erupt. Regardless, she was determined to ignore him. Searching through the tool box—which was meticulously organized, as she had come to expect from Grandpa Lee—she found a miscellaneous collection of items. Duct tape. A coil of heavy rope. A pack of water-proof matches. A first-aid kit. An umbrella. A box of ammunition for the Remington rifle.

Nick knelt next to her and began searching through the tool box, too. He didn't meet her gaze and he didn't speak, and that was okay by her.

They took several things out of the bin that might prove useful if they were delayed on their journey back to the house. They were limited by the capacity of their pockets, and her purse. She had a large collection of hand bags and wished she hadn't brought one of her smallest ones with her for this visit, but it was well past the time to worry about such things.

One of the items they took with them was a steel canteen already full of water. She cracked open the first-aid kit and found a sealed packet of aspirin. She put the tablet on her tongue and chased it down with a couple of small sips of water; the water was cool and tasted fresh. It was only mid-April, but the morning was humid and hot, and though it looked as if it might rain, the heat might only get worse as the day progressed.

"Take a drink, and take an aspirin." She offered the canteen and medicine to Nick. "You got banged up when we crashed and you don't want to get dehydrated out here, either."

"Thanks. Looks like Grandpa Lee was prepared for all sorts of situations, huh?" He laughed, but it was an anxious sound, devoid of amusement.

Amiya pressed her lips together. She felt terrible for Nick. If Grandpa Lee didn't make it home on his own, if he collapsed somewhere in the woods and they couldn't find him . . . she couldn't dwell on the idea. It was an outcome too awful to contemplate.

They got out of the truck. Thunder boomed, shaking the ground. A strong, cool breeze pushed through the foliage. Amiya felt the first cold drops of rain on her bare arms.

She opened the umbrella they had taken from the truck. Nick joined her underneath the protective canopy.

"Where to now?" Nick asked. "Since I've apparently been fired as the navigator."

She ignored the dig. "We stick to the road and retrace our steps. I think only one or two wrong turns put us in our current location here."

"What about my granddad? If he's wandered off the trail, we won't find him if we're staying on the road."

"We can keep an eye out for him, but honestly we need to stay the course. We're no help to him if we get lost, too, Nick."

Nick nodded tightly. She could surmise that he didn't like her plan, but that he would go along with it, albeit reluctantly.

They started off, walking side by side in the middle of the narrow dirt path, keeping underneath the umbrella. They advanced at a brisk pace, and Amiya was grateful that she had worn comfortable, flat-soled shoes. If she'd slipped on the cute open-toe sandals that she had originally considered, her feet would've begun paying the price.

The truck's tires had left behind a clear trail in the dirt. But as the rainfall strengthened to a torrential downpour, the dirt evolved to mud, forcing them to the grass at the edge of the lane. The tire tracks dissolved in the bubbling stew of raw earth and grit, and Amiya got a sinking feeling in her stomach.

Nothing, absolutely nothing, is going our way, she thought.

Lightning flashed through the forest. The day had been so crazy, she half-expected a lightning bolt to strike a tree and send smoking shards across their way.

Avoiding the mud in favor of the foliage that skirted the path slowed them down. By the time they reached a juncture of the roads, whatever tire tracks she had hoped to follow had been completely obliterated.

There were four intersecting lanes, all of them winding away in different directions, all of them so crowded by trees and flora it was impossible to get any sense of where they led.

"Which way did we turn?" she asked. "Do you remember?"

"Left?" He put his fingers against his forehead as if to massage forth the memory. "Yeah, left. So, to retrace our steps, we need to go that way." He gestured with his head.

Amiya had her own tattered recollection of the route they had taken and was relieved that his assessment matched hers. She adjusted the strap of the rifle hanging from her back.

"Let's go," she said, and started in the direction they had agreed upon.

But Nick didn't move. He stood rooted to the ground, staring along one of the other paths as rain bulleted over him.

"Nick? What's wrong?"

"This is crazy, but I think I saw someone."

"Grandpa Lee?"

Shaking his head, Nick swallowed, his Adam's apple bobbing. He looked at her. His eyes were wide with fear.

"I don't think we're alone out here."

14

Nick wasn't sure who he had seen, but it wasn't his grandfather. From a rain-blurred distance of perhaps a hundred yards, he couldn't discern all of the figure's details as it crossed the path. It had moved swiftly and appeared to be thinner than Grandpa Lee.

"It's raining," Amiya said. She edged closer, shielding him beneath the umbrella's canopy. "In these conditions, you might not have seen what you thought you did."

"I know what I saw. I saw a person running down there." He pointed, his finger shaking. "What if they have my granddad?"

"Jesus, Nick, really?" Amiya said. "That's ridiculous."

"It would explain why he's missing. He was unconscious before we wrecked and then when we woke up, he was gone. What if he didn't wake up and leave on his own?" He stopped pointing, made a fist, and shook it. "What if someone took him?"

"Who would be out here, except for us?" she asked. "This is private property and it's gated."

"It's a lot of land, so much undeveloped acreage that people could be living out here secretly, and my granddad might not know it. Fences, gates can be easily climbed. There could be squatters here . . . drifters."

He was standing so close to her that he could feel her sudden shiver, and the tremor passed through to him, too.

"The idea scares me," she said. "But I have to agree it's possible. Still, why take your grandfather and leave us alone? No one took my purse or your wallet."

"We need to go find out," he said. "I guess it's a good thing you brought the rifle."

"Hang on now. I'm not Calamity Jane. I've never shot anyone."

"If someone is keeping my grandpa, I'll gladly shoot them myself," Nick said, and meant it. "Give me the gun."

She unhooked the strap from around her shoulders and passed the firearm to him. He slipped on the strap, and, holding the rifle across his chest, he charged off without looking to confirm whether she was following him. It didn't matter to him if she joined him or not. He was convinced of what he'd seen, and equally convinced that whoever he'd seen would have knowledge of Grandpa Lee.

If someone hurts my granddad, I'll kill them.

He started at a brisk trot, damp grass swishing around his legs, shoes squishing through mud. Cold rain slanted into his eyes and trickled underneath the collar of his shirt. A few seconds later, Amiya caught up to him and put the umbrella over them.

He cast a sideways glance at her. "You believe me?"

She puffed out air. "I don't know, but if you're right, I'd never forgive myself for not doing everything I can to help."

She kept up with him as they jogged. Soon, they reached the approximate area in which Nick thought he had spotted the intruder.

"Look, there's a trail here." He pointed with the barrel of the gun. A narrow, muddy path branched off the main lane and snaked deep into the woods. The forest was so dense in that area that he couldn't view more than ten feet ahead. "I don't see any signs of where this leads."

"Have you ever been in this section?" Amiya asked.

"It's almost funny that you ask, 'cause when I think about it, Grandpa Lee *never* let me wander back here without him. Ever. That was an ironclad rule of my visits: never go off alone. He would take me to the lake, but that was all I ever saw. All of this land around us is uncharted territory to me."

"That's not reassuring in the least." She swept her gaze around warily and brought her attention back to the trail leading deeper in the wilderness.

Nick checked the rifle. Ready to rock.

"Stay behind me," he said.

They followed the trail into the forest.

15

Amiya hadn't truly accepted Nick's story of seeing a stranger slip into the woods. She believed he *thought* he had spotted someone, but her experience in psychology had proven that people viewed the world through an imperfect lens. Emotion, faulty memory, bias, and environmental factors influenced perceptions. It was the exact reason why eyewitness testimony was often discounted in criminal trials.

So when they had traveled along the trail for several minutes, brushing past brambles and vines—and then discovered actual evidence that they weren't alone, she found herself in the uncomfortable position of disbelieving her own eyes.

"What the . . . ?" Nick said, letting the sentence trail off unfinished.

Amiya, too, was silenced by what they'd found.

A makeshift campsite had been erected in a small clearing about twenty yards off the trail. A damp, tattered bedsheet had been tied between low-lying tree branches, providing a crude shelter. Raindrops escaped the tree canopy and beat a solemn cadence against the fabric.

Nearby, small chunks of wood had been gathered in a pile, evidently serving as kindling for a fire. The wood was charred and dusted with ashes.

Underneath the bedsheet roof, Amiya saw a dirty blanket full of holes.

"Someone's been living out here, in the woods, like a homeless person," Amiya said. She pursed her lips. "I'm trying to understand how this could be happening here."

"I bet it was the same person I saw," Nick said. His eyes looked haunted. He clutched the rifle against his chest. "But I don't see them now. They're gone."

Using a long tree branch she'd picked up off the ground, Amiya turned over the blanket. She found a decapitated doll's head underneath. The plastic face was smeared with dirt, the fake black hair full of dead leaves, and one eye was missing.

"This is a child's home." Amiya shook her head, trembling. "Probably a girl. My God. We've got to report this, Nick. This is terrible."

"Yeah." Nick lowered the rifle, breathing deeply.

With a scream, something dropped out of the trees and landed on Nick's back. Nick yelped in surprise and collapsed to his knees.

Amiya realized that the shrieking, attacking creature was a child. Wild-haired and dark-skinned, wearing only a filthy blue housedress, she was trying to stab Nick with a sharpened piece of wood.

"Get off him!" Amiya shouted.

She seized a fistful of the girl's dress. Baring her teeth, the girl swiped at her with the stake, drawing a searing cut across Amiya's forearm. Amiya cried out and pulled back.

Nick got his bearings and flipped the girl over his shoulders. The child tumbled against a tree, but bounced back onto her feet.

Like a feral feline, she hissed at them and brandished the stake.

Amiya estimated the child to be eleven or twelve years old. The poor girl was emaciated. The sodden dress hung on her bony frame like a shapeless sack. She wore a muddy pair of low-cut sneakers with ragged shoelaces. A weathered, small purse with a thin, fraying strap was slung across her chest.

Runaway, Amiya thought, and felt her heart kick. So much of her counseling work had been with young girls like this, victims of abusive households who often wound up trapped in the sordid world of underground sex trafficking. Amiya had seen it so many times, and it was always heartbreaking.

Fear glistened in the girl's penny-brown eyes, but there was a threat there, too. Amiya knew this child would not hesitate to strike at them again if she sensed danger.

"It's okay," Amiya said softly, but in a firm tone. She opened her hands to show they were empty. She was so focused on the girl she barely registered the bleeding cut on her arm. "We aren't here to hurt you." She glanced at Nick, who had already lowered the rifle. "You okay?"

"Yeah, got some nicks and scratches, nothing serious."

Nodding, Amiya turned back to the girl. She noticed some type of raised welt on the child's neck, a symbol that looked like a "W," and her stomach twisted.

She's been branded with a mark of ownership. Like property.

"My name is Amiya," she said, and tapped her chest. "This man here is my friend, Nick. What's your name?"

"The Overseer comes looking at night," the girl said, in a tremulous voice so soft Amiya could barely hear it over the pattering rainfall.

Amiya frowned. "Who is the Overseer?"

"Stay away from the plantation," the girl said, and cast a quick, terrified glance behind her.

"Plantation?" Nick asked.

"He has helpers." A tear tracked down the child's soot-filmed cheek. "If he catches you . . . you'll never leave."

"Have you seen my grandfather?" Nick asked. "He's very sick. He was wearing overalls and a hat."

Amiya thought she saw recognition spark in the child's frightened eyes.

"The Caretaker can't be touched," she said, and shook her head.

"You've seen him?" Amiya asked. "Where is he? He needs our help, honey."

In Nick's eagerness to get answers, he moved toward the girl. The girl drew backward like a startled animal.

"Hey, wait," Nick said.

"Get out!" she screamed. She whirled around and darted into the brush.

Amiya chased after her, Nick on her heels, but the girl moved like a zephyr and clearly knew her way through these woods. Within a minute, Amiya had lost track of her.

Amiya stopped running and leaned one hand against a tree trunk to aid her balance, her heart racing. Nick bent over next to her. He coughed, spat in the dirt, cursed.

"She knows about my grandpa," he said. He scowled, wiped rain out of his eyes.

Amiya had taken the first-aid kit from Grandpa Lee's pickup and fitted it in her purse. She took it out then, and used an antiseptic pad to clean the cut on her arm. She applied an adhesive bandage over the wound.

"She jabbed that stake at you a few times," Amiya said.

"I'm good," Nick said, waving off her help. "She called my grandpa 'the caretaker.' What the hell does that mean?"

"Not sure, and she said he can't be touched. I'm assuming he's off-limits to . . . someone? Everyone?"

"What was all that talk about an Overseer, and a plantation?" Nick asked.

"I was hoping you might have some idea. Does of any of that sound familiar?"

"All I know is that my ancestor was a slave here, and somehow got this property from his owner," Nick said. He shook his head. "I don't know if there was ever a plantation here. I've never seen it, and no one's ever said anything to me about it. I'm as clueless as you are."

"I don't think she was lying." Amiya shivered, hugged herself. "She was terrified."

"And the Overseer?" Nick said.

"Clearly, it's someone that frightens her. Most likely, it's the same individual who branded her on the neck with the letter 'W.'"

"Westbrook," Nick said, softly.

"Come again?"

"Grandpa Lee, he's always called this land 'Westbrook.' I thought it was only something he made up, but maybe it's not."

"Maybe the plantation is named Westbrook," Amiya said.

Both of them were silent for a moment. Amiya had always been uncomfortable with the idea of plantations. The very word "plantation" conjured lurid images and disturbing narratives of her ancestors bartered for and sold like common property, family members separated, women raped; shackled, whipped, forced to endure hard labor in sunbaked fields from dawn to dusk.

"We've got to find this place," Nick said. He swung the rifle around from where it hung across his back and into his hands. "Grandpa Lee could be there. If this girl was there, there could be others like her, too. Remember, she said this Overseer person has 'helpers.'"

"A helper could have taken your granddad, you think?" she asked.

"I'm convinced he didn't disappear on his own, whether she claims he can't be touched or not."

"I'm trying to understand how all of this could be going on here without your granddad's . . . consent," Amiya said, delicately. "A runaway child and some person who calls themselves an Overseer, all of this happening on his property? I'm struggling with this."

"What're you trying to say?" Nick glared at her. "You think he's in on it?"

"I can't imagine that Grandpa Lee is involved in anything as awful as this; I truly can't."

"But?" Nick asked.

"The child knew his identity, Nick. She had a name for him. I don't know the extent of his involvement, but he certainly hasn't been totally forthright with you."

"Fair enough." Nick grunted. "Then I think we'd better find him."

16

The rainfall had stopped, but the storm clouds remained behind, cloaking the day in a gloom that had penetrated the very core of Nick's spirit. Not long ago, he'd been optimistic that they would find their way back, that Grandpa Lee would have returned to his house, and they would drive him to the nearest hospital for medical attention, and everything would work out fine.

But all of those plans had collapsed, and they were lost, in every sense of the word.

Runaway children being kept prisoner on the property? Some guy who called himself the Overseer branding kids with a "W" and keeping them too terrified to escape, and employing a team of minions to assist his endeavors? A plantation being utilized for unknown purposes?

Worst of all, they still had no indication of what had happened to Grandpa Lee.

When the nameless girl had spoken of the plantation, Nick recalled that she had looked over her shoulder, as if the dreaded place were located somewhere behind her. He and Amiya took that as a clue for where to begin their search. The narrow dirt track continued on in that direction, too, winding through the thicket.

As they advanced along the muddy path, Nick glanced at Amiya and said, "We shouldn't have come here, Amiya. All of this that's going on, it's my fault."

Amiya sighed. "Whether we had come here today or not, Nick, there would still be a runaway child out here who needs help."

"But Grandpa Lee wouldn't be missing. That's on me. I . . . I pushed him too hard with that shit about selling the land."

"Not your finest moment, I agree."

"The timing was wrong. My approach was wrong. But I thought being direct was the best way to do it."

Amiya only shook her head. "You still don't get it."

"I have my reasons for wanting to sell. To be honest, after what we saw back there with the kid, I'm more motivated than ever to convince my granddad to sell this land. He doesn't even know what's going on out here, I'm convinced. But he could be held liable."

"We need to get the facts," she said. "At this point, we know so little we can't draw any conclusions, but we know there's a child here who needs our help, and your granddad does, too."

They pressed on. Although they couldn't get a signal on their phones, Nick was able to use his iPhone to check the time. It was almost noon. How many hours were there until sunset? Eight or so?

The Overseer comes looking at night.

The kid had freaked him out a little. He wanted to believe she was psychologically unstable and was either imagining or exaggerating some of the things she'd said. But this was his granddad's property—his *family's* land—and he had a rifle and was fully capable of using it to enforce his rights. If anyone was involved in some sort of criminal enterprise here, he was going to put a stop to it.

Although the rainfall had ceased, the humidity seemed to have increased, and the woods were beginning to feel as if they were steaming. Sweat saturated the back of Nick's neck and dripped down the channel of his spine. Beside him, Amiya pulled up her hair and knotted it in a quick ponytail.

"A cold shower would be nice, huh?" Nick said.

"Tell me about it. A big meal, a cold shower, and a long nap, in that exact order."

Nick was about to respond when he thought he heard something. He stopped in mid-step.

"What is it?" she asked.

"Running water," he said. "Hear it?"

"I think so." She cocked her head, listening. "Back in the day, plantations were often built near waterways. It could mean we're heading in the right direction."

They followed the trail around a bend, and soon discovered the source of the sound: a creek about twenty feet wide, full of fast-moving silver water and rocks. A felled elm tree spanned the width of the creek, and could serve as a crude bridge.

A gaggle of geese wandered along the edge of the muddy bank. They ratcheted their heads around at Nick and Amiya's approach, and squawked.

"Feels like we interrupted a private party," Nick said.

"The water is flowing from that direction." Amiya pointed to their left. Nick noticed that she had taken out her iPhone again and had accessed a compass app.

"You are quite the Girl Scout, babe," Nick said.

"I remember a few things from my troop days." Amiya smiled briefly, pointed to the left again. "That's north, the direction from which the water is flowing."

"I'm not sure where we are in relation to the lake we saw earlier," Nick said. "But I'm going to assume that this plantation will have been built close to the water source. We should head north."

They traveled in that direction, keeping close to the bank of the bubbling creek. The constant trickle of the running water had the weird effect of triggering Nick's thirst. Amiya lent him the small aluminum canteen that she had attached to her purse.

"Small sips, please," she said. "Although we're next to a creek, I doubt the water is safe to drink without boiling it first."

"If there truly is a plantation up here, there ought to be a well near it," he said.

"Among other things," she said with a sneer. "Like slave quarters and the big house."

The creek gradually widened, the water flowing with greater strength. About a hundred feet ahead, on the other side of the stream, Nick saw a wooden shed amongst the pines. The structure looked old, like a relic that should have been standing in a museum, or torn down.

"We've got something up there," Amiya said.

17

Upon closer inspection, the shed was in worse condition than Nick had initially thought. Once white, the paint had faded to a washed-out gray, much of it peeled away in the elements. Thick verdant vines snaked through gaps in the roof and the hinges of the closed door. A thatch of broken branches covered the top, like a bird's nest.

An old-fashioned padlock was still attached to the door hasp. The metal bristled with rust.

"There might be something useful in there," Amiya said.

Nick tugged at the lock and found it still functional. He hammered the butt of the rifle against the metal loop. It took three strong whacks to break it apart, each slam echoing through the woods like gunfire.

Amiya stepped forward and detached the busted lock from the hasp. She grasped the rusted door handle and pulled, but the tangle of vines and plants prevented her from getting it open more than a couple of inches.

"Let me help," Nick said.

Together, straining and grunting, they pried open the shed door, undergrowth tearing away like connective tissue. Something small, dark, and furry bolted from inside and rushed away through the tall grass. Amiya let out a short yelp of surprise.

Nick moved to get a better view of what lay inside. He gasped.

Two frayed ropes dangled from the ceiling of the structure, secured by iron bolts. The end of each was knotted around the wrists of a badly decomposed human corpse.

Each foot of the body was bound by rope, too, the ropes held by bolts on the floor.

Nausea whirled through Nick. He had to take a couple of steps back to regain his balance. Next to him, Amiya put her hand to her mouth.

"Torture," she said in a whisper. "Tied up in here and left to die."

Nick drew several deep breaths; it felt as if his stomach was going to empty its contents. Once he regained his bearings, he forced himself to move forward and take a closer look, but it felt as if lead weights had been strapped to his feet.

The corpse was too far gone for him to determine facial features, but it wore clothing. A badly soiled T-shirt that once had been white, and denim jeans. A pair of Nike sneakers, too, a style that had been popular perhaps five years ago.

Nick swallowed. "This person, they haven't been here that long. A few years at the most. The shoes aren't that old."

"Who imprisoned them in here?" Amiya asked. "The Overseer?"

Steeling himself, Nick edged closer. Black beetles and other burrowing insects had made a home in the orifices and crevices of the body.

"I could really use a pair of gloves right now," he said.

"Hey, don't," Amiya said.

Grimacing, he slipped his fingers into a front pocket. Something small and shiny scampered out of the folds of fabric, and Nick nearly gave up the effort. But a growing sense of duty compelled him forward.

This is my family's land . . . my responsibility.

The first pocket he checked was empty, but in the other front pocket, he grasped what felt like a wallet. He fished it out and backed away from the shed.

"Props to you. I couldn't have done that," Amiya said. "I know my limits."

The wallet was filmed with dried blood and the remnants of other fluids. It crackled as Nick spread it open in his hands.

Inside, Nick found several faded credit cards, the raised type so worn that he couldn't read the names on the front. He also discovered an expired South Carolina state ID card issued in the name of Joshua Turner. The photograph was hazy, but it looked like a dark-haired Caucasian male, and based on the birthdate he would have been twenty-five years old.

"How did this guy wind up here?" Nick asked. "I don't get it."

He handed the wallet to Amiya, who accepted it carefully, mindful of getting filth on her hands.

"He didn't go in the shed willingly, I promise you that," she said. "He was purposely confined in there. That's an act of pure evil."

"Unimaginable." Nick wiped sweat from his brow with the back of his hand and glanced at the corpse. "Bound in a hot, enclosed space, no water, no food—that would have been a prolonged, agonizing death."

"His family and friends probably still hope he'll come home someday," Amiya said. Sighing, she gave the wallet back to Nick. "How many others are here? I'm almost too afraid to find out."

Nick tucked the billfold in the young man's pocket. Together, he and Amiya pushed the door back into place. When this was all over —whatever *this* turned out to be—Nick planned to notify authorities of what they had found so the remains could be properly disposed and relatives notified.

"I just realized something," Nick said. "You'll think it's cold-blooded, but bear with me."

"What now?" she asked.

"We're not going to be able to sell this property for a fraction of the original asking price," he said. "People have been tortured and killed, runaway children are being branded and God knows what else. No one's going to pay top dollar for land where these things happened. It's like trying to sell a house after a homicide occurred there."

"I can't believe you're still thinking about the money, Nick." She looked at him as if he'd crawled from under a rock.

"I'm only stating a practical fact. I have to consider it."

"I don't want to hear about money anymore, okay?" She waved him off. "Let's keep moving."

18

Someone was chopping wood.

That was Nick's best assessment of the noise they heard after they had advanced through the forest for several minutes, after they'd left behind the horror in the shed. The distinctive sound of metal cleaving through wood occurred every ten seconds or so, with the predictable cadence of a metronome.

Thwack . . . thwack . . . thwack . . . thwack . . .

He and Amiya had kept close to the bank of the creek, on a northward trajectory. The noise seemed to issue from ahead, growing louder and sharper as they advanced.

"What do you think?" he asked Amiya. "Sounds like a woodcutter?"

"It's on our way." Anxiety clouded her eyes. "But considering what we've seen so far out here, we should be careful."

"No doubt." He swung the rifle around, into his hands. "Whoever's at work up there could know something about Grandpa Lee."

"And the girl we found," she said.

"Right, along with any others. We need someone to tell us what the hell is going on."

Tall weeds swept around their legs. A haze of gnats trailed them, dive-bombing his eyeballs with annoying persistence. Nick flicked his hand across his eyes to bat the insects away.

Nevertheless, as they trudged forward, Nick kept his gaze fastened on the surrounding woods, alert for anything out of the ordinary: a shirt, a hat, a face. The forestland had taken on a uniformity that made it impossible to distinguish one region from another. Any sign of a human would have stood out.

Thwack...thwack...thwack...thwack...

Nick stuck out his arm in front of Amiya. In a whisper, he said, "Hang on. I think I see someone."

Beside him, she studied the woods, lips pressed together as if she were holding her breath.

"Ahead on our right?" she asked.

"See the red-checkered shirt?" He pointed. "Maybe fifty yards out."

"Yeah." She wetted her lips, glanced at him. "So we take a slow approach?"

"Nice and slow. Let's see what he's doing, who might be with him."

She nodded. They crept forward at a deliberate pace, Nick in the lead. Branches snapped under his footsteps, and he winced, made a mental note to watch his step.

The woodcutter continued to split lengths of wood. Nick saw, not far from the worker, a ramshackle house even smaller than Grandpa Lee's residence, and in much worse condition. The shack was constructed of a miscellaneous assortment of boards, and slewed sideways. It seemed a strong breeze might blow it apart.

"See that house?" Nick asked. "Damn, who the hell are these people?"

"There's a wagon, too," Amiya said. "It looks like it's drawn by a horse, like something from a hundred years ago."

Nick saw it. It looked as if the wagon was half-filled with cords of wood. This woodcutter, whoever he was, was chopping wood to transport to another location. But to where? The plantation?

They had drawn within twenty or so yards of the worker and finally got a better look at him. Although they were at his back, their position gave them a good look at his overall profile. It was a man: he was slender, of average height, half of his face covered with a wild, rust-colored beard. He wore a dirty straw hat. His red-checkered shirt was spotted with holes, the ragged edges flowing over his waist. He wore mud-splattered denims and dusty work boots. He might have been any age between forty and seventy: his face was so covered with what looked like soot that it was difficult to be sure.

The man stopped chopping wood. He straightened, balanced the axe on his shoulder. He turned around.

Involuntarily, Nick did a sharp intake of air. "What the heck is wrong with his face?"

"Some kind of disfigurement," Amiya said, under her breath.

The man hadn't appeared to spot them. He wandered toward the shack. Ambling with a slight limp, he disappeared inside the house.

Nick had watched enough. He started forward.

"Hey," Amiya said.

"Listen, this is my family's land," Nick said. "I need an explanation for what this guy is doing here. This is trespassing."

"Okay, hang on." She caught up to him.

They came into the clearing where the man had been working. Ahead, in the dirt lane, the horse grumbled.

"Crazy," Nick said to himself.

The front door of the house was slightly ajar, but Nick didn't see the man or anyone else; it was too dark inside to make out anything from a distance. Nick approached.

"Hello!" he said. He kept his grip on the gun. "I'm Nick Alexander. My family owns this property. Is anyone here?"

"Hello!" Amiya called.

Nick reached the door's threshold, Amiya at his side. He rapped on the wood with his fist.

A hand emerged from the darkness and seized his wrist. Someone snatched him into the blackness.

Behind him, Amiya screamed.

19

Nick opened his eyes to find himself lying on his back, surrounded by pungent, chopped firewood and someone lying on top of him. He was in motion, the greenish canopy of trees above scrolling like dark clouds across a sky.

The person's head lay against his left shoulder, curly hair on his face. He recognized the fragrance of the shampoo and the texture of the hair.

Amiya.

He felt the slow rise and fall of her chest against his. She was alive but unconscious.

Their transport creaked and rocked. He heard the clop of hooves against dirt. He realized they had been placed in the wagon and were being taken . . . somewhere.

His head ached terribly. He couldn't remember much of what had happened, but he thought someone had smacked him hard with a blunt object. He felt a painful knot throbbing on his skull.

He tried to sit up. Although Amiya lay atop him, he felt restraints on his limbs: cold metal on his wrists, and something binding his legs at the ankles, too. Chains?

As he attempted to move, Amiya stirred, too. She lifted her head. Her gaze found his. A fearful confusion shone in her eyes.

"You okay?" he asked.

"Nick?" Her breath was hot against his cheek. "What happened?"

"We were ambushed, I think. Must've been that guy we saw, and someone else."

"Are these . . . chains?" She looked downward at her hands. "Oh my God."

"We're in the wagon, with the wood. Let's try to sit up."

She adjusted her body to give him space to maneuver and winced. "My head . . . it's killing me."

"We both took blows." Straining, fresh sweat popping out of his face, he forced himself upright into a sitting position.

Stacked lengths of chopped wood surrounded them. Heavy wrought iron shackles bound both of them at their wrists and ankles. The restraints were designed in a fashion that was popular a long time ago; he recognized the style from touring a museum.

During antebellum slavery times, he thought and felt a chill settle over him despite the day's warmth.

He swung around. Two people sat on the wagon's bench: the man in the red-checkered shirt, who held the reins of the horse, and who now happened to be strapped with Nick's rifle, the gun angled across his back; and a woman wearing a dusty, navy-blue dress, her steel-gray hair gathered in a bonnet.

As if she sensed his attention, the woman turned and looked at them. She had the weathered complexion of one who had done difficult, manual labor for a living. Her dark eyes were hard as stones. Wrinkles were etched deep into her sunbaked face.

A faded "W" was imprinted high on her forehead, like a birthmark.

"Settle down back there, y'all," she said, her words inflected with a thick South Georgia accent. She lifted a walking cane and shook it once at them. "Or I'll settle ya down again."

"My family owns this property!" Nick said.

"His grandfather is the Caretaker," Amiya added. "You shouldn't be doing this."

"That so?" The woman grinned, showing a mouthful of darkened, ruined teeth. "Oh, the Overseer's gonna be tickled by that, y'all being 'ssociated with the Caretaker. Indeed, he will."

Nick glanced at Amiya, and the fear in her eyes mirrored his own.

He tugged at the shackles, but it was pointless. The restraints were old, but held firm.

"I'm so thirsty," Amiya said, and he noticed that her lips were chapped. "They took my purse, all of our stuff."

"I can feel my wallet in my front pocket," Nick said. "Not that there's anything in there that'll do us any good."

"Like the man we found in the shed," Amiya said. "He had his, too."

"They take only useful items." Nick stared at the shackles on his wrists. "This morning I woke up in my house in Buckhead. Now I'm chained up like a slave riding in a wagon. Is this really happening? Is this not some elaborate hoax?"

"I don't think so, Nick," Amiya said. "Look up. We're going to the plantation."

20

A miya shared Nick's sense of displacement, that surreal feeling that they had fallen through a crack in their world and landed in a terrifying, alternate reality.

And the sight of the plantation mansion, more so than the old shackles on her feet, truly brought it home for her.

The mansion stood off in the distance, surrounded by pine trees. It was built in the Greek Revival style popular for wealthy landowners in the South during the antebellum era: a two-story, square-shaped structure fronted by thick Doric columns.

But this estate, as grand as it no doubt had once been, had devolved into extreme disrepair. Kudzu had invaded the residence, the vines climbing and coiling through every visible inch of the façade. The windows looked like empty eye sockets. A portion of the roof had collapsed.

"What the hell is that?" Nick said. "You think someone lives there?"

Amiya couldn't answer his question, her attention drawn to another region of the property, west of the estate: the fields.

Am I dreaming? she thought. *Please let it be so.*

The fields were pale green and she wasn't sure what crop had been cultivated, but people were out there working. She saw at least ten of them. They were too far away for her to discern the details of their appearance, or their activity. But they were stooped over, intent upon their labors, methodically working along rows of land.

"They're working like actual slaves," Nick said, and it sounded as if he'd been slugged in the stomach.

He reached for her hands, and despite their shackles, she clasped his hands in hers, tightly. She and Nick had experienced their share of disagreements this day, but he was the only thing in this new reality that seemed real; the only thing she understood.

She pulled him closer to her, their noses nearly touching.

"No matter what, we've got to stick together," she said.

"We will. Promise."

The wagon veered off to the right, away from the mansion and fields, and toward a barn so dilapidated it was a miracle it was still standing. The horse drew to a stop in front of the barn doors.

"Where are you taking us?" Nick asked.

"Bringin' you in the barn here, fella," the man said, speaking for the first time. He ambled around the side of the wagon, the old woman at his side. He held the rifle he'd taken from them, and from the casual ease of his grip Amiya didn't doubt he knew how to use it. His beard was so thick and unkempt that it looked as if a red-haired furry animal had attached itself to his face, but Amiya saw that "W" etched above an eyebrow like an old scar.

"You got the brawny look of a field hand we can use out here," he said.

"Field hand?" Nick stared at them, mouth open in disbelief. "This is insane. This is my family's property. I told you that!"

"That don't mean nothin' to me." The man spat in the dirt.

"We want to speak to the person in charge here," Amiya said, in the most forceful tone she could muster. "We want to talk to the Overseer."

"Nah, you don't," the man said. Something that looked like fear flashed in his eyes.

"Where is the Overseer?" Amiya said. "Take us to him. Please."

"Ain't you just a little firecracker?" The old woman reached out to touch Amiya's hair. Amiya jerked away from her hand. The woman grinned like a snake. "We gonna take you up to the big house, gal. You way too pretty to be workin' outside. I think you just his type."

"Keep your hands off me," Amiya said, but a fresh, cold current of fear had washed over her. *Whose type?*

"Listen to me, both of you, please," Nick said. "Obviously, neither of you want to be here, either. You've been branded. Take us back to my granddad's house. We can all leave this place, every one of us."

Amiya hoped that Nick's appeal to reason would have gained some ground with them, but both the man and woman laughed. Their laughter carried a note of anxiety, however, and she realized: *They want to leave, too, but they're afraid.*

But what could they have been afraid of? The Overseer wasn't present, and they had their own means of transportation. What stopped them from taking that horse and wagon and driving right out of there for good?

"You want to leave, don't you?" she said, and looked from the man to the woman. "Why can't you? What's keeping you here?"

"That's enough talkin'," the man said. "We got to get y'all settled in. Go on, now, Betty. Let's get 'er done."

The old woman—Amiya figured her name was Betty—lowered the gate of the wagon. She reached for Nick.

"Come on," Nick said. "You don't need to separate us. It's not necessary."

"Yeah, it is." The bearded man raised the rifle and pointed the barrel in their direction. "Those is the rules—we got to organize y'all 'corrding to function. Don't fight it 'cause I don't wanna hurt ya."

"Please, don't do this." Amiya turned her attention to Betty. Hot tears had begun to leak from her eyes, and the chains rattled as she extended her arms in a gesture of desperate supplication. "I'm begging you. Please, let us stay together."

But Betty's jaw was rigid, her lips turned down in a sour expression as if she'd been asked to swallow a rotted lemon.

"Rules is rules," she said. "We all gotta abide by 'em."

Betty seized Nick by the ankles and pulled. Nick tried to twist away. The man edged closer to the wagon and levered the rifle inches away from Nick's head. Nick froze.

Amiya held her breath, tears dripping down her face and into her lap.

"That's enough from you," the man said. "Let Betty get you outta there."

Shaking, Nick turned to Amiya. His eyes glistened with unshed tears, but she saw a degree of resolve in his gaze that she had never seen before, and it made her heart clutch, for at that moment, she realized how much she loved him, despite everything.

"I'll come find you," he said. "Promise."

And they dragged him away.

21

———————

The helpers shoved Nick into the humid darkness of the barn, and it sounded as if they slammed bolts over the doors. They hadn't bothered to remove his restraints. He staggered, wove drunkenly, and with a rattle of chains, finally collapsed onto what felt like a pile of hay.

The barn wasn't entirely dark. In his peripheral vision, he sensed a window above the doorway, high and out of reach. A shaft of gray afternoon light came through the gap and brightened a section of the floor nearby.

Fatigue got the best of him; he didn't understand why he was tired, but it was impossible to resist, his eyelids sliding shut almost automatically. He faded into sleep . . .

He dreamed of Grandpa Lee. They were riding in the pickup truck, just the two of them, and his grandfather was driving.

They were rolling down a wide dirt lane, the sun at their backs. The dilapidated plantation mansion loomed directly ahead of them.

"Welcome to Westbrook," Grandpa Lee said. He winked. "It's not much to look at during the day, son, but at night . . ." He whistled and shook his head. "It's a sight to behold."

"Why didn't you tell me about this place before?" Nick asked.

"It wasn't your time," Grandpa Lee said. "I wasn't sure you wanted to take on the duties, anyway. You never come around to see me."

"What duties?"

"I'm the Caretaker, son," Grandpa Lee said. "This ground is cursed with old magic, but someone's gotta take the weight."

Nick didn't understand his grandfather's remarks, and in the fluidly shifting nature of dreams, he was suddenly somewhere else. In a barn, at dusk. He was naked, and felt hay bristling at his back.

Amiya was on top of him, nude like he was, and she was riding him with an enthusiasm that bordered on desperation.

A "W" was branded on her cheek, like a tribal scar.

"We don't have much time—gotta make every second count," she whispered.

She raised her arms above her head, her breasts hanging in his face like sweet melons, and he saw that shackles bound her wrists. He reached up to caress her breasts. Chains linked his wrists, too.

"I love you, babe," he said, thrusting into her.

The scene dissolved. He was still in the barn, but on his feet. Amiya was gone. He was alone.

Well, perhaps not completely alone.

The barn door had been opened. Full dark waited outside. He heard the clop-clop-clop of a horse's hooves striking dirt, the sound drawing closer to the doorway.

He wanted to run and hide, but his hands had been chained to a thick wooden post. He pulled against it, and the metal bands bit into his wrists, didn't let go.

The horse arrived at the doorway. Its rider sat atop, his face cloaked in darkness, but Nick had an impression of immense size and power.

Raw terror came over Nick like a tight hood.

"It's your time," the Overseer said, and his voice was in Nick's head, echoing in Nick's blood.

The Overseer dismounted and approached the doorway, moving

like a shadow. In one gigantic, gloved hand, he held a whip. The whip writhed across the ground like a living serpent, and Nick saw, incredibly, that it had a hinged mouth embedded at the tip, and that mouth was full of razor-sharp fangs.

In his other hand, he held a branding iron that glowed like the sun.

"You will never leave . . ."

Nick came awake with a cry bursting from his parched throat.

Panting, he looked around, blinking. While asleep, he had rolled onto his back. He saw dusty rafters far above, a wood ceiling, and a square of gray light.

He was still in the barn.

He shifted, the shackles clanking with his movement.

He was still restrained, too.

"No," he said, tears streaming down his cheeks. He shook his head. "No, no, no."

He'd wanted to believe it had all been a dream, that he would awake in his home in Buckhead, perhaps dozing away the afternoon on his plush sofa, and he would get up and text Amiya and she would say she was on her way, and couldn't wait to see him.

He screamed. The sound came out as a hoarse, ragged shout.

He was dehydrated. His tongue felt like sandpaper, and his lips burned.

Groaning, he sat up. His hands tingled, and he wriggled his fingers to restore his blood circulation.

He had to find some water, somewhere.

He had to get out of here, take off these shackles, find Amiya and Grandpa Lee, return to civilization, and report what was going on.

The possibility of selling this property, which as early as this morning had seemed within his grasp, now felt like a pipe dream, as unlikely as him winning a multi-state lottery jackpot. No one would ever want this land once the truth broke out.

This ground is cursed with old magic . . .

The figment from his dream spun through his thoughts like a

scrap of windblown paper. Was it something cooked up by his fear-blasted subconscious mind? Or a hint of a deeper truth?

He struggled to his feet, needing to take his time lest the shackles throw him off balance. His joints ached and crackled.

The humid air was still. The smells of hay and sweetly decaying wood permeated his nostrils. A lone fly orbited his head.

The afternoon light sifting through the window relieved some of the shadows in the chamber. He was alone in the barn. A rickety wooden ladder led to a loft area, but the window, which had no glass, was far out of reach above the doorway. Scattered bits of straw covered sections of the floor. The back wall was solid wood, leaving him with only the front door as a possible exit route.

A steel pail stood beside the doorway. He shuffled toward it, his chains clinking.

The bucket was half full of cool water. Carefully, he lifted it off the floor, levered the cold rim against his lips, and sipped.

He didn't know how long the water had been standing in that pail, but it tasted great. He drank deeply, until his throat was lubricated and the coolness had spread throughout his limbs. As he bent to place it back on the floor, he inadvertently tipped it over. The remaining water spilled across the dirt.

"Dammit."

He set the bucket upright but it was a pointless effort. He could hope only that the long drink he'd enjoyed sustained him—

—until the Overseer comes—

—until he found a way to get out of the barn.

The sliding barn door had a long, rusted handle. It didn't budge, despite him pushing against it with both hands and leveraging all of his weight. He remembered seeing bolts on the exterior. They had secured it in place.

He kicked the door, out of sheer anger. It barely rattled in the frame, and for his outburst, he was rewarded by losing his balance. He dropped to his butt in the hay, the impact banging through his tailbone. He cursed, tears of pain leaking from the corners of his eyes.

It was tempting to lie back in the hay and wait this out. Eventually, someone would open the door and let him out of here, possibly this Overseer guy. Perhaps he could talk sensibly to the Overseer.

But he remembered the fear that had flashed in the bearded man's eyes at the mention of an audience with the Overseer, remembered the ugly brands that all these people had been forced to bear. Would a man who applied a hot iron to bare flesh be willing to talk sensibly?

And where had they taken Amiya? *I think you just his type*, the old woman had said to her.

Nick forced himself back to his feet.

He shuffled around the perimeter of the barn. He searched for weaknesses in the walls: a loose board, a gap he could exploit. Although the barn was old and in generally poor condition, he didn't see a way out, not without the aid of some kind of tool.

He looked up. The window was out of range. Was there anything useful in the hayloft?

He approached the ladder. A couple of rungs were missing, but enough were within his reach for him to climb. He began to ascend. It was a challenge with the shackles. He had to coordinate the movements of his hands and feet or risk tumbling back to the floor.

Straining and grunting, he finally reached the loft.

The wood creaked under his weight. The air up here near the ceiling was so thick and hot it was difficult to draw breath; it wrung fresh perspiration from his pores.

The area measured perhaps ten feet wide and eight feet long. He discovered another pile of hay, gathered together in the shape of a crude bed. A tattered, soiled pillow bleeding tufts of cotton.

Someone else was here, too.

He lifted the pillow, but underneath found only more strands of hay.

What did you think you would find, Nick? A conveniently hidden crowbar?

He laughed at the fatal absurdity of his predicament. Salty sweat rolled into his eyes, mingling with the tears that had begun to stream down his face.

Keep moving, Nick; keep looking. Or go to sleep and wake up when it's time to get branded.

Descending the ladder was harder than climbing it, and on the way down, when he was about seven feet above the floor, he missed a rung. Luckily, he landed on his feet a few feet away from the ladder, in a bed of straw—and thought he heard something metallic shift in the thin stalks.

He bent over and searched the area, snatching away straw like a kid tearing wrapping paper off a gift.

He couldn't believe what he found, buried at the bottom of the pile.

An old, rusted claw hammer.

22

They had separated her and Nick, but Amiya refused to yield. She was determined to fight her situation at every turn, to claw and tear—literally, if necessary—until she brought this living nightmare to an end.

As the wagon took her away from the barn where they had imprisoned Nick, and along the winding dirt road toward the run-down mansion, Amiya screamed at her captors. She berated them as cowards. Called them idiots. Told them they would be sorry for what they were doing.

The nameless man, and Betty, ignored her. Despite her shackles, she had wriggled around amidst the lengths of wood, positioned herself to have a full forward view as the wagon advanced across the plantation. The man kept urging the old horse along, and Betty didn't so much as turn to look at her.

Neither did anyone else.

The path to the estate trailed along the edges of the cultivated fields. She got a closer look at the people working out there—the so-called "field hands."

The first thing she noticed was the ethnic diversity of the prisoners. There were about twelve of them, and they were Black, White, Asian, Latino. Mostly men; she saw only two women. All of them wore clothes that hung on them like rags, but there was no uniformity to the clothing. One guy had on a tattered throwback basketball jersey. Someone else wore a T-shirt turned brown with dirt. One of the women wore a flower-patterned blouse but the flowers had turned gray.

None of them bothered to look in Amiya's direction. They seemed, in fact, to deliberately avoid glancing at her, as if merely looking her way would have brought corporal punishment.

But she didn't see anyone supervising their work, no slave driver demanding they continue to labor under threat of a whip. They were almost zombielike in their demeanor.

"What's the matter with you all?" Amiya shouted. She raised her chained hands and shook them, the chains rattling loudly enough for the noise to carry across the field. "Someone, please, help me!"

She might as well have been pleading with androids programmed to perform a single task and nothing else. Her pleadings brought no attention.

She could see that "W" branded on a few of them: at the back of their sweat-saturated necks, on their foreheads or cheeks. No doubt, all of them bore the mark on various regions of their bodies.

But a mere symbol could not have compelled the degree of terrified obedience that these people displayed. These people obviously had been broken, through systematic torture and brainwashing. What else could have forced someone in modern-day America to submit to slavery on a decaying southern plantation?

The road took them around the back of the estate. The wagon clattered to a stop underneath the boughs of a gigantic magnolia tree.

Amiya saw a frayed rope swinging from a thick tree branch overhead. Although she immediately realized what sort of punishment that noose probably had been used to deliver, her rational mind struggled to accept it.

Hangings going on out here? I can't believe this.

But it was as real as the cold perspiration creeping down her spine. People were dying here. Both she and Nick could die here, and who was around to prevent it?

None of her friends or family knew exactly where she had gone. They knew only that she was spending time with her boyfriend, as usual—she and Nick practically lived together already. Nick's mother would have known where they were, but how long before she became alarmed and notified the authorities? Nick wasn't a teenager under the close observation of helicopter parents. He was a forty-year-old man, and his mother might not note his absence for days.

They might not last for days out here.

They say the Overseer arrives at night—what will he do to us when he comes?

Betty and the man ambled around to the rear of the wagon. Amiya glared at them.

"Don't touch me," she said.

"This one here, now she's a little pistol, Jimmy," Betty said. "I might need you to help me here."

"She ain't gon' do nothing," Jimmy said. He carried the rifle loosely. "She like a cute little dog. All bark and no bite."

Oh yeah? Amiya thought. *Try me.*

"You gonna behave, gal?" Betty lowered the back of the wagon.

Amiya bunched her hands into fists and had drawn up her legs. "Where are you taking me?"

"Up there in the big house. You gon' be under Miss Lula's charge," Betty said.

"Who is Miss Lula?"

"Miss Lula runs the house staff," Betty said.

"That house? It's falling apart. How can anyone be living here? The place looks like it needs to be demolished."

Betty and Jimmy both snickered, as if they were in on a private joke.

"You'll see for yourself at sundown," Betty said. She reached for Amiya's legs. "Come on now, gal."

Amiya thrust her legs, kicking Betty's outstretched arms. Betty grimaced with pain.

"Help me with her, Jimmy," she said. "Don't bruise her face. She's pretty and you know how he likes 'em."

With a grunt, Jimmy clambered onto the wagon.

"Get away from me!" Amiya screamed. She swung her legs toward Jimmy, trying to sweep his ankles and topple him over. He climbed up on a pile of wood, out of reach. She twisted around, swinging her hands, but he was nimble on his feet and got behind her. He hooked his hands in her armpits and lifted her.

"No, no, no!" Amiya shrieked and squirmed.

"Calm down, gal. Good Lord," Betty said. Amiya kicked, but Betty got her hands around her ankles, above the shackles, and her grip was strong. "You gon' live like a princess up in here so long as you behave—better than what most folks here get."

"Ain't that the truth," Jimmy said.

They dragged her, screaming, out of the wagon, across a threadbare section of yard, through a doorway in the rear of the house, and into a shadow-filled room. Though her tears and tangled hair, Amiya saw a sagging ceiling, floorboards buckled as if something had broken up from underneath them, peeling dirty wallpaper. Gray afternoon light filtered inside through a pair of boarded-up windows. She smelled rotted wood and mildew, and her stomach lurched.

They placed her on a thin, lumpy mattress that lay in the corner of the room. Yawning, Jimmy sauntered back toward the doorway. Amiya tried to get up, and Betty shoved her back to the mattress and wagged her finger in her face.

"You settle down, you hear?" Betty said. "I'm warnin' you for your own good. Miss Lula ain't got as much patience as me."

"I need water." Amiya coughed. "Please."

Betty opened a metal flask that she wore attached to her leather belt. She brought the rim to Amiya's lips.

"Sip slow now," Betty said.

Amiya drank. The cool water helped to quell the nausea that had threatened to overtake her.

As she held the flask to Amiya's mouth, Betty brushed locks of hair away from Amiya's brow and studied her face.

"Quite the stunner you are," Betty said. She clucked her tongue. "All that smooth skin—looks like you got a nice figure on you, too. Hmph. Hard to say where you'll get your mark."

"No one's marking me," Amiya said, mouth half-full of water. She swallowed, glowered at the woman. "I'll die before that happens."

Betty pursed her lips, took away the flask, screwed the cap back on.

"That might be a blessing, honey," she said.

They left her in the room, shutting the door as they departed. She heard their footsteps receding, wooden floorboards creaking under their weight.

Silence fell over the house. She heard random pings and groans, noises that old homes tended to make, but she didn't hear voices or any sounds of human activity.

Gathering her strength, she wobbled to her feet. She stumbled to the doorway, barely able to keep her balance with her chained ankles, carefully avoiding the ruptured sections of the floor.

It was an old door, fashioned of heavy oak, with a faded, old-fashioned brass knob. She turned the knob. She heard a mechanism creak inside, but she couldn't open the door. It was secured from outside the room.

She hammered her fists against the wood.

"Help!" she shouted. "Someone, please help!"

No answer. She hadn't expected a response. If there were others in the house—a house staff, as Betty had stated—they were deaf to her pleas, like the prisoners outdoors.

She turned away from the door and assessed the room for anything useful.

It was a small chamber, and held only a meager amount of

furnishings. A brass chandelier, festooned with cobwebs, hung askew from the high ceiling, dangling from a rusted length of chain. Against one wall stood a battered chest of drawers, all of the drawers missing. A padded chair sat underneath a boarded-up window, dirty stuffing spilling out of the seat cushion like entrails from a wounded beast.

Nothing in here's going to help me.

Tears dripped from her eyes, and she felt a sob building in her chest that threatened to overcome her. She lowered her head and willed herself to breathe slowly.

She had to stay strong, focused on escape. Despair was her enemy. If she allowed her resolve to weaken, she would be vulnerable to whatever methods they employed to break and mold their prisoners.

But she was so exhausted. That lumpy mattress lying on the dusty floor was beginning to look as inviting as the queen-size Tempur-Pedic bed in her condo.

I've gotta stay in motion.

Although none of the furnishings in the chamber seemed helpful, to keep herself active, she opted to take a closer examination of each of them. She began with the chest of drawers. It was literally an antique, and in terrible condition; it looked as if it had tumbled end over end down a long flight of stairs.

Using both hands, she gripped the edge of the dresser and nudged it away from the wall. It was heavier than it looked, and she couldn't manage to move it more than a few inches, the furniture legs screeching against the hardwood floor as she pushed. Breathing hard, she peered into the shadowed gap between the dresser and wall. She saw only dusty spiderwebs.

Next, she examined the chair, pulled it away from its position, and found nothing. She climbed onto the chair and pried at the slats of wood that had been nailed across the window, but they held firm.

She was too tired to bother trying the other window. Sighing, she eased onto the ruptured cushion to catch her breath. She hung her head, gazing at the shackles on her wrists and ankles.

As much as she hated it, she was inclined to accept that there was no way out of this room, no way out of her restraints, and nothing to do except wait for an opportunity to escape.

Up there in the big house, you gon' be under Miss Lula's charge . . . Miss Lula ain't got as much patience as me . . .

Amiya clenched her hands into fists.

I will resist, she thought. *Until my dying breath.*

But until then, she did something she hadn't done in years: she prayed.

23

The hammer Nick had discovered buried in the pile of hay wasn't mantled with rust, as he had initially thought.

In the deepening afternoon light, he saw that it was covered in blood. The dried blood fluttered away in brittle flakes as he ran his thumb across the surface.

He tried to piece together what might have happened.

Had someone used the hammer as a weapon? Against whom? The Overseer? Or perhaps one of the "helpers" had used it to punish one of their captives.

Clutching the wooden handle in both hands, he surveyed the barn walls, trying to remember where he had found those loose boards. He lurched toward the wall, chains rattling.

He located the most promising section in a far corner near the back wall. There, several boards had warped and revealed a slice of daylight a couple of inches wide. He inserted the claw side of the hammer head, adjusted to get some leverage, and pushed.

Wood groaned and creaked, and the gap widened.

He wiped sweat from his brow with the back of his wrist. He

slipped the claw into another loose section and pushed again, his arms trembling from the effort, his chains clinking.

A rusted nail popped out, rolled into the dirt. The gap was about six inches wide, large enough to admit his foot. He bent close to the opening he'd created and peered outside.

He saw tall, thick weeds, and the sweet fragrance of wildflowers swirled around his head.

Encouraged, he pried loose another slat of decaying wood, tossed it aside. Then he peeled back another one and knocked it away. After he had loosened yet another piece, he estimated that he had enough space to squeeze through. He lowered himself into a crawl.

Behind him, the barn door rattled.

Nick froze, his heart pounding. Half-heartedly, he thought he could try to fit through the gap he had made, but he knew intuitively that he would never make it. One of the helpers would see him trying to wriggle through, grab his ankles, and reel him back in.

The door swung open, and in that rush of sudden brightness, Nick saw a slight, familiar figure slip inside and shut the door.

"Hey, Mr. Nick," a soft voice said, in a whisper.

It was the girl that he and Amiya had encountered earlier in the woods. The runaway.

Clutching the hammer, unsure of her intentions, Nick rose. "Over here."

The girl hurried toward him, her footsteps feather-light across the straw.

"What're you doing in here?" he asked.

Anxiety glimmered in her eyes, but she met his gaze without looking away, and he realized in that moment that she was older than she looked.

"I'm helping you escape." She took a small silver item from her dress pocket that looked like a key. "We've gotta hurry. I think one of the field hands saw me come in here, and they can't be trusted. They'll snitch to a helper in a New York minute."

Nick blinked. The sudden turn of events had made him dizzy. "I, uh, had opened up a hole, here."

"We might still need to use it. Quick, give me your hands."

He offered her his shackled wrists. Using her key, she unlocked one restraint, and then the other. Then she knelt and disengaged the shackles on his feet.

"I don't even know how to thank you," he said, massaging his chafed wrists.

For the first time she offered a brief smile. "I'm Raven, by the way. Don't thank me until we get clear of the plantation."

"I can't leave without my girlfriend, Amiya. They took her away to—"

"They took her to the big house; I saw it," Raven said. "I can't sneak in there—it's too dangerous. We'll have to figure out something else, but first we need to get off the plantation."

"How old are you, anyway?"

"I'm seventeen." She gave him a challenging glare. "Please, no snide remarks about how I look like a little kid. I've heard them my entire life and I'm not in the mood. Now let's *move*."

She grabbed one of his hands as if he were a child and tugged him toward the barn door. The door rattled, and Raven halted in midstep, spun, and pushed Nick in the back.

"Go through the hole you made," she whispered. "Hurry, hurry."

Nick slipped the hammer into a belt loop of his Levi's. Getting low to the ground, in a crab-walk stance, he scrambled forward. His knee joints popped like firecrackers. Straw spun in his face. He reached the gap in the boards just as the barn door banged open.

"I know y'all in here," a male voice said. "You can't run off. Come on out."

"Keep moving," Raven whispered, nudging him forward.

Nick crawled forward on his hands and knees, the edges of the boards scraping against his shoulders and back. A splinter speared his neck, and he bit his tongue to hold back a cry. He wove into the tall weeds on the other side.

Raven slipped through the hole after him as quick as a shadow, fitted one of the boards back into place.

"That'll do for a little bit," she said, coming beside him. "Stay low to the ground. The weeds will give us some cover."

"Where are we going?" he asked.

"Just follow me." She grabbed his hand again, as if he were a child who needed to be led. "Let's go."

24

Nick realized that Raven had mastered the layout of the plantation. Crouching, warning him to stay low, she took him without hesitation to a small shed-like building standing in a grove of pine trees. They took cover behind the structure.

"Stay down," she whispered. "Someone's close."

Nick heard footsteps crunching through the grass. Someone muttered and cut wind. Nick scowled as the stench reached his nostrils and held back a cough. Raven wrinkled her nose.

After a half minute or so, the searcher moved on through the weeds.

From there, Raven guided him in another direction, into a region thick with trees and undergrowth. Off in the distance, Nick saw a row of three nearly identical squat, ramshackle log cabins.

"Are those slave quarters?" He pointed.

"People I know live there." She tugged his hand. "We've got to put some more distance between us and the plantation. They're going to be looking for you."

"Who will? These helpers?"

"Yeah, until sunset." Her brows furrowed with worry. "Then *he* comes."

"The Overseer," Nick said.

She nodded. "We need to get your girlfriend out of the house before then. Come on, keep moving. I'll tell you what I know once we're clear of this place."

She led him deeper into the forest. It was an area he hadn't encountered before, but that wasn't saying much. Everything he had seen during the past few hours was new to him, a troubling mystery unfolding in literally the backyard of his childhood. *I've been coming here to see Grandpa Lee since I was a kid, and never knew any of this was back here*, he kept thinking. *If my grandpa knew about it, why did he hide it from me?*

He worried about his grandfather. He knew Amiya was in the house, but where was Grandpa Lee? Was he somewhere safe? Had he recovered from his medical crisis?

The helpers, Betty and that other guy, had confiscated his cell phone. He wished he still had it, even if he couldn't raise a signal. He would have liked to at least try to reach someone in the outside world: his mom, Omar, anyone. The more time he spent in these backwoods, imprisoned in this bizarre environment with its own set of rules and its own strange hierarchy, the less connected he felt to the modern life he had always known.

Insects buzzed around him. It was getting later in the afternoon, but the onslaught of heat had continued. Traveling through the forest was like swimming in a steam bath.

He was starving, too. He hadn't eaten anything since breakfast that morning.

He studied Raven as she led him through the woods, her petite but strong hand hooked over his. She said she was seventeen, and he believed she might be, but based on her been-there, done-that demeanor she could have been older. He wondered about the horrors she had witnessed here.

More than anything else, he wondered why she stayed.

They neared the creek, and Nick began to recognize his surroundings again. Raven had just taken them on a different route to the water. She released his hand, picked her way down the muddy bank to the water, knelt, and cupped both hands in the stream. She splashed water over her face, took deep sips.

"That water's not safe to drink," Nick said. "You should boil it first."

"This might be the only water you get for a while." She drank from the bowl of her hands. "I've got bigger issues to worry about than catching a few germs."

Nick looked around, reassured himself that they had lost their pursuers. He joined Raven at the creek's edge. The stream looked clean, but that meant nothing; earning a doctorate in a field of scientific study had filled his mind with all sorts of disturbing facts about what likely lurked in this water.

But he was thirsty. Escaping through the steaming woods had wrung buckets of sweat from his pores. His risk of severe dehydration was more pressing than the likelihood of ingesting harmful parasites.

He dipped his fingers in the creek, found the water cool. He formed a cup with his hand and sipped. It had an earthy flavor, but otherwise tasted fine.

Raven watched him. "Good, huh?"

"Do you have anything to eat?" he asked. "I'm starving."

"When was the last time you ate something?" Her eyes narrowed.

"This morning, breakfast. Why?"

"What did you eat?" she asked.

"We went to Starbucks. I had a breakfast sandwich—it had an egg, bacon, and cheese. I had a cup of yogurt, too."

"Wow, that sounds so good." She closed her eyes, licked her lips. "If you ate like that just this morning, you aren't starving. Not yet."

He frowned. "Well, what the hell do you eat, then?"

"Whatever I can find." She stared at him. "Some of these trees out here have fruit and berries. I've learned which ones make me sick and which ones are okay to eat."

"That's it? Damn, no wonder you're so thin."

"I've killed rabbits a few times," she said, lifting her chin proudly. "I started fires and cooked them on it. It was a lot of work, but it was *so* good."

"Foraging for berries, hunting rabbits with sharpened sticks . . . that's no way for a girl your age to live," he said. "You ought to be graduating high school and prepping for college, Raven."

"Tell me about it." She gave him a hard look. "I'm doing what I can just to survive."

Nick took another sip of water, cleared a large rock on the bank, and sat on it.

"I don't understand what's going on out here," he said. "Tell me everything you know. Please."

Raven glanced around them and peered at the sky, as if reassuring herself that it was okay to let her guard down.

Then she found a rock near his, eased onto it, and started talking.

25

Amiya nodded off. She hadn't planned to slip into unconsciousness, but the fear gnawing at her had worn her out, and before she realized it, she had slumped over in the chair and fallen asleep.

She had a disturbing dream. She was still in the decrepit plantation house. She was in one of the musty bedrooms, and her arms were stretched above her and chained at the wrists while she hung from a wooden beam. Completely nude, she shivered as a cold draft gusted through a broken window.

Then a man appeared in the room, in the shifty nature of dreams. He looked as if he had risen from a grave. Clumps of dirt crumbled from his shoes, his eye sockets were empty, and his gray face was like a fright mask. He lumbered toward her and pawed her breasts with his ice-cold hands, and a raw, pink tongue poked from between his dead lips and rotted teeth.

"I am well pleased," he said. "Y'all done good, girls . . ."

Amiya snapped awake with a short cry.

She had tipped over in the chair and fallen asleep while lying against one of its upholstered arms. Blinking, she sat up. Her head throbbed, and she was still wearing the cold shackles on her wrists and ankles.

Grayish light sifted into the room. She was unsure how long she had been asleep, but it was still daytime.

Still time, she thought.

Footsteps creaked against the floor, coming from outside the room.

She tensed, all of her drowsiness washing away in an instant. She glanced around the room for a weapon, remembered she had already looked and found nothing at all.

The only weapon she would possess was her own mind. She would have to keep her composure and use her brain to figure out a way to gain the upper hand against these disturbed people.

Someone unlocked the door. It swung open on noisy hinges.

A tall, husky Black woman with a light beige complexion stepped inside. Amiya guessed she was in her mid-fifties, but it was difficult to be sure. She wore a faded green housedress and scuffed, flat-soled black shoes. Her auburn hair was pinned up in a bun and emphasized the severity of her sharp-edged features.

She had eyes the color of faded pennies. With a slow, measuring gaze, she assessed Amiya.

Without any introduction, Amiya realized that this was Miss Lula.

"Betty was right about you," the woman said and gave a brief, satisfied nod. She sounded like a stern schoolteacher, someone who would send you to detention for a minor infraction. "A lady like you has no place outside. You got a name?"

"Amiya." She swallowed. "Amiya Turner."

"I'm Miss Lula. I'm in charge of the house." Miss Lula shuffled toward her, favoring her right leg. She fished a set of keys out of her pocket. "Betty says you're a little pistol."

"I don't want to be here," Amiya said. She had to fight to hold back a cry. "I want to go home."

"I won't tolerate disobedience," Miss Lula said in a tone that brooked no argument. "Stand up."

Amiya rose, shakily. She almost toppled over, had to lean against the chair to support herself.

Miss Lula knelt and inserted one of her keys in the shackles on Amiya's ankles. As she bent over, Amiya saw the back of her neck and recognized the faded "W" branded on her flesh.

How long has she been here? Years? Why don't any of these people leave?

Miss Lula disengaged the restraints on both of her ankles, rose, and unlocked the ones on Amiya's wrists, too.

"Thank you, ma'am," Amiya said, and massaged her chafed skin.

Something that looked like approval glinted in Miss Lula's gaze.

"Keep that up, and you'll do fine here, lady," Miss Lula said. "Let's go get you a bath and some appropriate attire."

As desperate as she was to get out of there, the idea of taking a bath, washing away the grime and dried sweat that filmed her skin from the day's accumulated horrors, seemed like an invitation to go to a spa.

"That sounds good," Amiya said. "Is there anything to eat and drink?"

"Of course. You'll get the best we've got to offer, and no less. It's what your role requires."

Amiya was afraid to ask her next question, but she couldn't let it go: "What is my role?"

Miss Lula smiled at her. She had perfect teeth, Amiya noted.

"Betty didn't tell you?" Miss Lula asked. "You're going to be the Master's mistress."

26

_____

"I ran away from home," Raven said. Sitting on the rock, she gazed into the bubbling creek, but to Nick, her eyes seemed to be focused on a faraway place. "I grew up in Charlotte. North Carolina." She laughed, but it was a sour sound. "Had the bright idea that I would run away to Disney World, in Orlando. I'd live with Minnie Mouse and the Disney princesses, like Tiana and Merida. How stupid, right?" She glanced at Nick but didn't wait for a reply before she continued. "I was thirteen, totally naïve, but I knew I _had_ to get away."

"Get away from where you lived?" Nick asked in a soft tone.

"My mom's boyfriend. He was more interested in me than he was in her, I guess. I told her about it after he came into my room one night and got in bed with me, and touched me in my private places. You know what my mom said? She said I was jealous and didn't want her to be happy, that I was trying to steal her man."

Nick felt ill. "I'm so sorry."

"It got worse from there, with him. He knew he could do whatever he wanted and my mom wouldn't believe me. I had saved up some money in a piggy bank so I left, took the bus. I had enough bus fare to get me to Atlanta. I guess I should have stayed there, I had some cousins there, but I didn't know how to get in touch with them, and I didn't totally trust them anyway. I thought they'd turn me in to my mom. So I hitched some rides. All I had to do was smile at these guys and bat my eyelashes and they would take me with them. See?"

She smiled at Nick, demonstrating, and despite her bedraggled condition, he could understand how she had been able to successfully charm her way into vehicles with men who ought to have known better.

"But you didn't make it to Orlando," he said.

"My last ride, he had to drop me off outside of Macon, he said, because he had to go home to his wife. I had to start walking. I thought I'd just run into another guy at a gas station or something. But . . ." Her voice trailed off.

"But what?" he asked.

"To you, this will sound crazy because you don't understand this place . . . but I was *drawn* here, like this." She pantomimed a fisherman reeling in a fish.

"Drawn here? Like this place was some kind of magnet?"

"Right!" She snapped her fingers. "I was passing by, on the road that I remember outside here, and I heard things coming from here, amazing things, and I got closer and saw the big fence."

"There's a 'No Trespassing' sign on the fence. And the fence surrounds the entire property."

"But I *heard* things coming from here. Kids laughing. Families having fun. People singing. It sounded like—"

"Disney World," Nick said, and felt a coldness rush through him.

"Like a carnival, a fun place." She nodded, her eyes sparkling, as if she were still enchanted by the memory.

"I went through this weird gap in the fence, sort of like a magic door, 'cause it just appeared all of a sudden," Raven said. "I kept hearing that carnival, just ahead, and smelling delicious food, and I saw a Ferris wheel—seriously. It sounds so stupid to say it now. It's obvious this place tricked me. But that's what was there back then, as clear as this water running through the creek." She stuck her hand in the brook and splashed water on her fingers.

Nick didn't know what to think about her story. What she claimed was absurd and impossible. But if she had given him her correct age—seventeen—that meant she had been on the land for four years (if she even knew how to keep track of time), living in deplorable conditions. Psychologically, such a life would have had a damaging effect on her critical faculties.

(But why did I feel a chill?)

And in such a state of mind, she could believe that she had really been drawn here because it had seemed as if a magical amusement park lay just ahead.

"Anyway, one of the helpers found me and took me to the big house," she said. "It definitely wasn't that amazing castle you see in all those Disney movies." She laughed, a bitter sound. "Not during the day anyway."

"How did the others wind up here?" he asked. "Any idea?"

"We all have our own stories, I guess, but everyone who's told me how they got here, they seemed to be going through tough times, too, whenever they got close to this place. Homeless or depressed, or whatever. And they heard or saw different things than I did. It's like the land knows what we want deep down, and it uses that to *call* us . . . to lure us onto the property." She shuddered.

"Who are these so-called helpers? Tell me about them."

"They're like the slaves on Westbrook. Well, I guess they were slaves at first, but they're different. Like, upgraded."

"Upgraded?"

"They're stronger—a *lot* stronger." She rolled up the sleeve of her dress and showed him her scrawny arm. He could see faded fingerprints on her forearm. "I got this from when Miss Lula grabbed me. She didn't like how I was cleaning the kitchen and I got stupid and gave her some lip."

"Who is Miss Lula?" he asked.

"She runs the house. Crazy mean, but she comes off nice at first —until you piss her off. I really hope your girlfriend doesn't make her mad. She'll be sorry. Miss Lula ain't no joke."

Nick had to pull his thoughts away from the danger Amiya was in, or else he would go nuts with worry and lose his focus. Focus, he realized, would be key to them getting out of here.

"I need to understand this place, Westbrook," Nick said. He wished he had a pad and pencil to keep all of his facts in order. "We have the helpers, okay. The ones who picked me up, Betty and some guy—"

"Jimmy," Raven said. "I was watching."

"Jimmy," Nick said. "He's a helper. How many helpers are there, total?"

"Seven," she said. "I know all of them. I know their routines. I have to, to stay away from them."

"You escaped," he said.

"Five months ago. I keep track of the days in my head. I got away a hundred and fifty-five days ago and I've been here at Westbrook for one thousand, four hundred, and seventy-two days. I've always had a good memory for numbers."

Nick nodded, impressed. "How did you get out and get keys to the chains?"

"I had help, inside," she said. "One of the other house slaves, we came up with a plan. He didn't make it . . . the Overseer caught him." She shivered, and glanced nervously at the sky.

"Who is the Overseer? Every time someone brings up this person they get scared, and supposedly he comes out at night?"

"I've only seen him once," she said. "At sundown, I go into a hiding place and I don't come out 'til morning."

"But *who* is he?" He was struggling to temper his frustration with her nonsensical replies.

"I don't know. He marked me—that's the one time I saw him." She tapped her head, the wound of the old scar on her face. "He's the one who does the marking of everyone. The mark keeps you here."

"It's just a symbol on your skin," Nick said. "Hell, I have a buddy in a frat who got branded when he pledged. It's not keeping you bound to this place, Raven."

"You don't understand." She only shook her head. "But you don't have the mark yet, and neither does your girlfriend. That means you can get away—and maybe you can help me get away, too."

Of course, Nick realized. *That's why she's helping us. She thinks we can help her escape.*

These people, these helpers, the so-called Overseer . . . they had done one hell of a mind job on Raven and the others. To have influenced these captives to actually believe they couldn't escape because of a mark on their skin? It was one of the most insidious cases of brainwashing he'd ever seen.

"I need to understand how my grandfather plays into this," Nick said. "You called him the Caretaker?"

"No one's supposed to touch the Caretaker," she said. "Not even the Overseer or the Master, I think."

"Jesus, now we have a master, too?" He laughed. "This is too much, seriously. The master lives in the big house, huh?"

"Exactly." Raven didn't laugh. "I think they took your girlfriend to be the Master's mistress."

Nick's laughter died in his throat. "His mistress? What?"

"The Overseer runs Westbrook, but the Master still lives in the house. Like the Overseer, he comes around at night. Wakes up, I guess. All he seems to care about are the women. He never bothered me. I guess I wasn't his type."

Nick was trying and failing to wrap his mind around the outpouring of information. "What does he do with the women?"

"Whatever he wants," Raven said, plainly. "They don't have much choice about it, either."

Focus, Nick thought, though he felt almost paralyzed with worry for Amiya. *Find out what I need to know and make a plan.*

"Back to my grandpa, the Caretaker. Have you ever seen him? Did he ever come around the plantation?"

"He lives over the bridge," Raven said. "I can't cross over the bridge because I have the mark—no one can, except maybe the Overseer. But I saw the Caretaker in other places, not on the plantation but around the lake. Like I said, you can't talk to him. I never tried."

"If you had talked to my granddad, he would have helped you leave this place," Nick said. "I've known him my entire life. He's a good man."

Raven shook her head, smiled sadly.

"The Caretaker knows about all of us," she said. "But he won't help us."

Nick was tempted to argue with her that Grandpa Lee could not have possibly known what was going on back there, but he had an uneasiness in his stomach about voicing such words. The truth was, his granddad must have known. The question was: Why did he allow it?

"My granddad is around here somewhere," Nick said. "I need to find him, and I need to get Amiya out of the house."

"Before dark," Raven said.

"Can you help me?" he asked.

She picked up a pebble, got to her feet. She tossed the rock across the creek, making it skip across the short span of water.

Finally, she glanced at him. "You think I'm crazy. You don't believe half of what I told you."

"I think you've been through a lot, Raven. You've lived out here for four years. I think you have a distorted perception of things."

"I wish," she said, and turned away. She tossed another pebble into the water. "But I can show you something that'll change your mind. Come on."

27

R aven took him to the bridge.

Nick always remembered the old wooden bridge, which spanned a narrow ribbon of stream, as being the entrance to "Westbrook proper," as his grandfather routinely explained it. Earlier, before all of this madness descended on them, he and Amiya had struggled to find their way back to it. Raven guided him through the woods and to the crossing easily; within fifteen minutes, the wooden structure was within sight.

"You really know your way around out here," he said.

"I don't have a choice," she said. "I have to stay ahead of the helpers and the Overseer. I use the trees to mark my way."

She pointed out miniature carvings on the tree trunks. He had seen those marks before and hadn't paid them much attention, figuring they had been created by animals pecking at the wood.

"Smart," he said. "So you've got your own navigation system."

"Sort of." She shrugged. "Came from necessity, I guess."

"Once we cross that bridge, I can get help for us," he said. "I can get back to my grandpa's house, get to my truck, and go to the police.

We can put an end to everything here: this plantation, the Overseer, the helpers . . . you'll be free."

"I won't be able to leave," she said. "But maybe you can get help for us, like you said."

As they closed in on the bridge, his spirits soared. He increased his pace from a brisk walk to a jog, shoes scraping across the dirt lane. He should have been exhausted after the day's struggles, but hope had given him newfound energy.

Raven tried to keep up but soon fell behind him.

"Come on!" he said, urging her along. "We're almost there!"

He reached the bridge, the wood creaking under his weight. Slowing, he turned to find Raven had drawn to a stop. She eyed the crossing warily, avoided setting her feet on the wood, and wouldn't touch the railing either.

Nick was halfway across. "Raven, let's go. It's okay."

"I wanted to show you this." She glanced at him, fear brimming in her eyes. She peeled back a lock of hair, giving him a full view of the mark branded on her face. "Watch."

"Come on, don't be ridiculous—" he started to say, and then he lost his words.

Wincing, Raven had placed one foot on the bridge, and the "W" on her face was glowing. It reminded Nick of the heat conducting tubes of a toaster oven when the power had been switched on: the mark, a ruddy orange, steadily grew brighter, and brighter.

Can't be seeing this. It's not really happening . . .

"See?" Raven stared at Nick, tears running down her cheeks. She put one hand on the railing, and the glowing suddenly increased in intensity, and Nick saw smoke tendrils rising from her face. She screamed at him. "See!"

"Stop it!" Nick broke his paralysis and pushed her away from the bridge. Raven staggered, dropped to her knees. She covered her face, trembling.

"Let me . . . let me take a look, please," he said gently. He knelt next to her. "Please."

Sniffling, she took away her hands. The mark had lost its unearthly glow, but it looked raw and sore, as if recently applied by the branding iron, and he caught a faint, sickening smell of seared flesh.

She gave him a baleful look. "You believe me now?"

"Raven, I'm a scientist," he said. "But what I just saw . . . I don't have a scientific explanation for it. Spontaneous human combustion triggered by touching something—nothing like this has ever been recorded."

"Help me get away from here," she said. She wiped tears from her eyes with the sleeve of her dress. "Help all of us."

He drew in deep breaths. If what she had told him about the power of the mark was real, as he had witnessed with his own eyes . . . he could not contemplate the implications of such a thing at the moment. He knew only that he needed to help her, and Amiya, and everyone else being held there against their will.

He looked skyward. He estimated that it was edging toward late afternoon. Perhaps a couple of hours left until sunset.

"You wait here," he said. "I'll be back for you—for all of you."

28

Nick crossed over the bridge, leaving Raven behind, the girl watching him with glassy eyes full of hope. She had given him the details on a rendezvous point if she was forced to slip out of the vicinity, but she warned him, again, about the looming threat of nightfall.

"Get back before dark," she said, and hugged him, surprising him. "No matter what."

"Promise," he said.

A keen sense of urgency pushed him into a run as he traveled the narrow dirt lane. He pumped his arms and legs.

He kept seeing that glowing mark on Raven's face, his brain trying to process how such a thing was possible, and finding no answers.

It is what it is, his mother liked to say. Sometimes you didn't have to understand the how or even the why of a thing in order to take the appropriate action. You had only to accept it and conduct yourself accordingly. *It is what it is.*

The lane diverged into a couple of different paths, but Nick had a simple landmark to guide him in that area. Peering down one lane, he saw, at the periphery, the boxy shape and triangular roof of his grand-father's smokehouse.

"Thank God," he said. The sight of the beloved structure was as welcome a vision as dry land might have been to a sailor lost at sea. He ached to be anchored back in the world he knew and understood.

He raced down the path, ghosts of dirt pluming from his rapid footsteps. Arriving at the perimeter of the home place, he looked around.

His Range Rover was parked exactly where he had left it: under-neath the wooden carport. He felt in his pocket, found he still had the key fob, too. The helpers had confiscated the rifle, but had left him with his wallet and keys.

He scrambled to the vehicle. As he rounded the back end, he mashed the fob, and the doors unlocked.

"Hold it right there, son," a familiar voice said.

Nick turned around to the house.

Grandpa Lee stood on the veranda.

He aimed a shotgun at Nick.

29

M iss Lula led Amiya through the house. If Amiya had found it challenging to believe before she had been inside that people had lived in such a place, receiving a brief tour of the interior of the mansion had impressed that sense of disbelief on her more strongly than ever.

Wax candles provided light, and showed beyond a doubt: the place was falling apart. The wide entry hall had gaps in the floorboards, and several sections had caved in, dropping down into musty blackness. Chandeliers teetered from rusted chains or had crashed to the floor altogether. The wallpaper was peeling away from the walls in desiccated strips.

"You live in here?" Amiya asked Miss Lula, who was proceeding through the wreck of a home with an air of indifference.

"All of us do," Miss Lula said. She glanced over her shoulder, eyebrows arched. "So will you, lady."

To hell you say, Amiya thought, but she didn't dare to speak the sentiment. Miss Lula had the frosty air of an old-school disciplinarian who wouldn't hesitate to smack you across the face if you voiced a cross word. The woman had yet to show her anything but mild civility, but Amiya was a keen judge of character—her work as a psychologist required it—and being in Miss Lula's presence kept her on guard.

She saw others in the rooms they passed. Mostly women, but she did see two meek-looking men. None of them spoke to her, but all of them were engaged in tasks so pointless that it seemed the height of absurdity. Scrubbing floors. Folding linens. Washing clothes in a big basin. Delicious aromas wafted from one of the rooms they walked past, and Amiya reasoned that it had to be the kitchen.

"Something sure smells good," she said. Her stomach growled.

"You'll eat after you bathe and dress," Miss Lula said.

She brought Amiya to a grand spiral staircase—well, it used to be grand. To Amiya, those canted risers looked like an accident waiting to happen. Part of the balustrade had actually peeled away from the staircase.

"Watch yourself, lady," Miss Lula said. She gathered the hem of her dress in her big fist and began to ascend the steps. The staircase groaned and popped under her weight.

Amiya hesitated at the foot of the stairs. She looked for a safe path and didn't see one.

"Don't make me ask you twice," Miss Lula said.

Amiya drew in a ragged breath, went up. She tried to follow the exact same route Miss Lula had taken, but it still felt as perilous as walking a plank on a pirate ship, and as she neared the landing, she lost her balance.

Cat-quick, Miss Lula reached out and grabbed her arm. She steadied Amiya and pulled her up as if Amiya weighed no more than a child.

"Thanks," Amiya said.

Miss Lula nodded, released her hold on her.

She grabbed me as if it were nothing, Amiya thought. *How could anyone be that strong?*

The second floor of the mansion was just as dilapidated as the ground level. More broken chandeliers. A damaged floor. Ancient peeling wallpaper. Warped doors sagging on hinges. Cobwebs everywhere.

They passed musty bedrooms, stepped past an old painting that had crashed to the floor. Amiya glanced at the painting: it looked like a depiction of the plantation, Westbrook, in its former state of grandeur.

She coughed against a veil of dust that passed over her. She followed Miss Lula to a room near the end of the long corridor.

"You'll bathe in here," Miss Lula said, pointing.

Amiya looked inside: no one ever would have mistaken the chamber for a spa, but it wasn't as bad as she'd thought it would be. A fat candle glowed on an end table, casting dim light over the smallish room. A porcelain claw-foot tub stood in the middle. It had been filled about three-quarters full with steaming water. A nearby table held a bar of soap, a sponge, and a thick white towel. A freshly cut red rose bristled from a faded vase.

"It's nice," Amiya said, and actually meant it.

"Like I said, you get the best we've got, lady," Miss Lula said. She took a bathrobe from a hook on the sagging door. "Go ahead and take off your clothes."

"Can I get a little privacy?" Amiya asked. "Please?"

"I'm not going anywhere." Miss Lula stared at her, and didn't leave the doorway. "You haven't been marked yet. There's no telling what you might try."

"All righty, then," Amiya said. "So this is going to be like high school gym class all over again."

Miss Lula didn't respond to the remark, and showed no inclination to turn around. Amiya stepped past her, moved near the bathtub. Putting one hand against the rim of the tub for balance, she peeled off her shoes, then her socks.

"You've had a pedicure recently, huh?" Miss Lula looked at Amiya's feet. "Red polish, no chipped paint."

"Right, last weekend, for all the good it'll do me now. I'll probably have blisters from all the physical activity I've had today."

Miss Lula kept staring at her feet. Her tongue poked out, swiped across her lips as if she were thirsty. Her gaze traveled up the rest of Amiya's body, and there was no mistaking the interest simmering in her eyes.

So it's this kind of party, Amiya thought, and was surprised at how little it bothered her. Perhaps because it was something that, finally, she could understand. If Miss Lula secretly craved to see some bare skin, she could give her a show. She could give her a show she would never forget—and try to find a way to use it to her advantage.

Not until your survival is at stake do you realize what you might be willing to do to stay alive . . .

Taking her time, Amiya unbuckled her belt. Miss Lula watched her, her hands clasped together so tightly in front of her it was as if she were trying to keep them under control. Amiya turned around, putting her back to the woman. She bent over slightly at the waist, slowly rolled down her pants.

She heard Miss Lula pull in a quick breath and whisper, "Lord have mercy."

Amiya tried to conceal her own trembling. She had Miss Lula heading in the right direction, but she had to play this carefully. If she hit a false note, or overplayed her hand, it would all blow up in her face.

"There's a zipper at the back of my blouse," Amiya said. She glanced over her shoulder, offered a demure smile. "Can you help me with it, please?"

Miss Lula hesitated as if she didn't trust herself, but her eagerness got the better of her and she came into the room, her shadow falling over Amiya. She fumbled with the blouse's zipper, managed to tug it down the track. Amiya could hear the woman's quivering breaths.

Amiya turned around. Miss Lula stepped back, but remained close by. Amiya slipped the blouse over her head and let it drop to the floor. Miss Lula's gaze never left Amiya's chest.

Amiya unhooked her bra, slowly let the cups fall away. Casually, purposely avoiding Miss Lula's eyes, she took her breasts in her hands, kneaded them a bit as if testing their firmness.

She stole a glance at her captive audience. A glistening film of sweat had moistened Miss Lula's forehead. *Good.*

Amiya peeled down her panties and kicked them aside, too. Turning sideways, she stretched her arms above her head like a lazy, sunbathing cat. Miss Lula's gaze was so hot Amiya thought she could feel it on her skin, like a heat lamp.

Under any other circumstances, Amiya would have been ashamed of herself. She knew that people found her attractive. She'd been getting compliments on her looks since she was a teenager, but she had never been one to use her physical assets to gain an advantage. She always strived to get ahead by using her intelligence, personality, and hard work.

But if she had to use her body as a weapon to secure her eventual freedom, so be it.

After she had given Miss Lula enough of an eyeful to guarantee the woman a couple of restless nights, Amiya climbed into the tub. The water had cooled a bit, but still felt amazing.

"Oh, I forgot the soap and sponge," Amiya said. "Can you please bring those to me?"

Miss Lula hurried forward and picked up the items from the end table. She placed them on the edge of the tub and waited there, hesitant.

"Thank you," Amiya said. "Gosh, I'm really sore. So much activity today."

She raised one leg out of the tub, water cascading along her thigh. Slowly, she flexed her muscles, letting out a soft moan that wasn't entirely false.

Miss Lula was entranced.

Flexing her thigh again, Amiya asked, "Can you help soap my legs, please?"

She knew she was playing with fire then, but she needed to tease Miss Lula just a bit more to ensure the woman's cooperation.

Miss Lula was kneeling at the edge of the tub before Amiya could finish her request.

"I wouldn't normally do something like this," Miss Lula said. "I'm not supposed to touch the ladies."

"It's only a bath," Amiya said. She lifted her other leg out of the water, wriggled her toes, stretched her calf muscle. Miss Lula followed every movement with keen interest. "It's no big deal."

Miss Lula pulled her gaze away, looked behind them at the doorway.

"You can't tell anyone I touched you," Miss Lula said.

"It'll be our little secret," Amiya said.

Miss Lula took one of Amiya's legs in her hands, ran her fingers along her skin. Amiya could feel the woman's hands trembling, and despite herself she felt a twinge of power.

Carefully, as if handling a delicate piece of crystal, Miss Lula took the bar of soap and slid it across Amiya's thigh, down to her calf, ankle, and foot.

"You are such a lovely woman," Miss Lula said in a hushed tone. "We've never had anyone quite like you here. You're like a perfect, beautiful doll."

"How long have you been here, Miss Lula?"

A shadow came over Miss Lula's eyes. "I shouldn't tell you about that."

"Our little secret, right?"

Miss Lula deliberated for a few heartbeats. "I can't remember how long. That is the honest answer. I wish I could, but I can't."

"Have you ever wanted to leave?" Amiya asked.

Miss Lula's gaze drilled into her. In a tight voice she said, "I love Westbrook. You'll also learn to love it here if you know what's good for you."

"I don't think I can ever learn to love a life of slavery," Amiya said.

She recognized she was treading close to the line, and for a moment it seemed like Miss Lula would erupt, but having her hands on Amiya's flesh seemed to pull her back from the brink. She reached for Amiya's other thigh, soap in hand. Amiya let her have it, to reel her back under her control.

"Lady, your life here will be the envy of every other resident of Westbrook," Miss Lula said. "You don't understand how fortunate you are, the blessings you'll receive."

The blessings? This woman was so far gone that Amiya struggled to think of an adequate response.

"I don't want to stay here," Amiya said. She hesitated, then: "I'm not entirely convinced that you do, either. We could get away together, you and me."

It was the wrong thing to say, and the instant the words left her lips, Amiya realized the gravity of her error.

"No one leaves Westbrook!" Miss Lula shouted, nostrils flaring.

Amiya cringed. "I'm sorry. I didn't mean to upset you."

Eyes flashing crazily, Miss Lula seized a fistful of Amiya's hair. Amiya screamed. Snarling, Miss Lula shoved Amiya's head underwater.

Amiya spluttered, warm water invading her nostrils and pouring down her throat. She fought to get up, to get air, but Miss Lula had her head pinned down beneath the surface, her arm as rigid as a steel pole.

Amiya's lungs burned, limbs thrashing.

I'm going to die here, drowned in a bathtub in the middle of nowhere...

When blackness had begun to seep into the edges of her vision, Miss Lula suddenly let her go. Flailing, Amiya broke the surface. She gagged, coughed, drew her wet hair away from her eyes.

Miss Lula had gotten to her feet. With a sneer, she tossed the bathrobe toward Amiya and turned around.

"That will never happen again, you filthy little temptress," she said. "Now, get dressed."

30

Nick had seen some unbelievable things happen that day. The incident with Raven back at the bridge when her mark had emitted an unearthly glow had been at the top of his list of unbelievable events.

That was until he saw Grandpa Lee emerge from the house pointing a shotgun at him.

His grandfather looked unwell. His eyes were deeply bloodshot, and his dark complexion was ashen. Dirt smudged his overalls, and Nick saw drops of crimson on his shirt.

But Grandpa Lee's grip on the gun didn't waver.

"I can't let you leave, son," Grandpa Lee said in a taut voice on the verge of breaking. "I can't let you bring in folks from the outside."

Nick struggled to pull his gaze away from the shotgun. The barrel seemed as dark as the abyss.

"Grandpa, you're sick," Nick said. "You had a seizure, possibly heart failure. I'm stunned that you made it back home."

"I've always been tough." Grandpa Lee lifted his broad chin with evident pride. "I was out for a bit, but I got it together. Hell, I was 'bout to go back to fetch you and your gal, 'til you showed up here."

"Can you please lower the gun?" Nick asked. "Can we talk, please?"

"Put down the car keys." Grandpa Lee motioned with the gun. "Toss 'em onto the porch."

Nick obeyed, the fob clattering onto the floorboards next to the mud-covered boots Grandpa Lee still wore.

"Okay?" Nick asked, hands raised.

Grandpa Lee lowered the shotgun slowly. Nick wondered if his granddad really would have shot him and decided it was wise that he hadn't pushed it. Grandpa Lee wasn't in his right frame of mind.

"Come have a seat on the porch." Grandpa Lee shuffled to one of the Adirondack chairs and eased onto it carefully. He angled the gun across his lap.

Nick took the chair next to him. "Grandpa, we need to get you to a hospital. You collapsed out there."

"That's enough of that, son. I'm not going anywhere. Neither are you right now."

"All right, I'll drop it," Nick said, but he felt dizzy. He clasped his hands in his lap as if to stabilize himself. "You know what Amiya and I saw out there? Are you willing to talk about that?"

His grandfather grunted. He removed his glasses and massaged the bridge of his nose. "I never wanted you to know, not until it was time, not until after we had prepared you."

"Prepared me for what?"

"The truth," Grandpa Lee said. He slipped his spectacles back on, his gaze sharpening. "Westbrook is cursed, son. The land, the people, everything on it, it's all cursed. Including me."

Grandpa Lee wiped his lips with a blood-spotted handkerchief and added, "Including you."

31

At any other time, Nick would have dismissed Grandpa Lee's words as the demented ramblings of a man suffering from a deteriorating mental condition. Curses? In the twenty-first century? But his grandfather's demeanor was grave, and though he was unwell, the alertness in his eyes was impossible to discount. He was telling Nick what he believed to be the truth.

"I don't understand," Nick said.

"We can thank our ancestor John." Grandpa Lee looked away toward his garden. He coughed once into his handkerchief. "He took on the burden, he bore the weight, and that weight has been passed down the family's bloodline. It finally fell into my hands. It was gonna fall into your mother's. Then on to you."

"The weight of what?" Nick asked. "Those people out there in Westbrook, they call you the Caretaker."

"Because *I have the burden*," Grandpa Lee said. He leaned forward, resting against his knees, and gestured wildly. "I keep out the outside. I live out here with no phone, no electricity, nothing except for what I can put together with my bare hands. I don't sell. I *can't* sell. You know what kind of offers I've gotten, son?" Grandpa

Lee cackled. "You think I want to be here? I could be living out my golden years on a beach somewhere, but I'm here, keeping all this mess pent up, keeping it safe."

"How are you keeping it safe if people are getting sucked into this place?" Nick asked.

"I can't do nothin' 'bout that." Grandpa Lee shook his head. "If someone gets too close, the land chooses 'em. It chooses whomever it wants."

They had gotten no closer to Nick really understanding anything. Nick felt as if he could scream. He shot to his feet, paced back and forth across the porch. Grandpa Lee merely watched him, sighed.

"None of this makes much sense to me," Nick said. "But I know people are living out there in squalor, Grandpa. They want to leave, and they can't because someone branded a mark on their bodies. These are innocent people who got tricked into coming here somehow. And now Amiya is there in the house, too."

"Y'all wandered off," Grandpa Lee said. "After you wrecked my truck, I got up—it took me a while to get my bearings—and I roamed around a little, not thinking straight, but then I came back to the truck, and y'all were gone. I would have gotten you out."

"We were looking for you!" Nick sucked in a breath, tried to calm himself. "Now Amiya is trapped there, like a prisoner. I have to get her out of there, and I need to free those innocent people living there like slaves."

"You remind me of myself, son," Grandpa Lee said. He shook his head sadly. "Big, brave ideas to set everyone free. I tried that, too. I'd convinced a handful of them that I could get them out. Do you know what happened?"

Nick stopped pacing, lips pressed together. He didn't need his granddad to tell him.

"Poof!" Grandpa Lee said, punctuating the word with a snap of his fingers. "When we tried to cross that bridge, they went off like firecrackers, five people, gone like that, and it was all on me, son—I'd might as well have shot them in the head myself. If you bring in the outside folks, the police, when they try to remove those poor people from Westbrook—"

"They'll all die," Nick said, and lowered his head.

"You have to take off the curse," Grandpa Lee said. "That's the only way to set them free."

Nick sat back in the chair and turned to his granddad.

"How do I do that, then?" he asked.

"You have to kill him," Grandpa Lee said.

"Who?" Nick said, but his gut had tightened, and he was convinced he knew the answer.

The Overseer.

Glancing warily at the late afternoon sky, Grandpa Lee rose from his chair. He hefted the shotgun over his shoulder and shuffled to the front door.

"It's gonna be dark soon," Grandpa Lee said. "You'll need to be on your way. Let's get inside and I'll tell you what I can."

32

The clock above the fireplace mantel read half-past five in the afternoon. Nick and Amiya had arrived there that morning around nine o'clock, meaning they had spent about eight hours there.

To Nick, it felt like eight days.

He didn't have access to a sunset calendar, but in mid-April, he believed that dusk would settle around eight that evening. Nightfall would arrive in less than three hours.

Then the Overseer rises...

The two of them sat at the small kitchen table. Grandpa Lee lit a candle and placed it in the center, giving the shadowed chamber the atmosphere of a midnight séance. He had brewed a pot of coffee on the wood-burning stove and set a chunk of hard bread and a slab of cured pork on a wooden platter at the table's edge. Nick poured himself a steaming mug of coffee and tore into the meat and bread between sips.

"They call him the Overseer." Grandpa Lee sat across from him, his face in alternating layers of shadow and light. "He's not like any of the others. He was there in the beginning."

"You mean when Westbrook, the plantation, was founded," Nick said.

Grandpa Lee grunted. "Eighteen twenty-three."

"I see." Nick didn't know what else to say.

"I know you're a man of science, son." Grandpa Lee sipped a bit of coffee and puckered his lips. "You're thinking, how could a man who was living in the early 1800s still be walking this earth? I appreciate science, too, but Westbrook has nothing to do with such things."

"I saw what happened when someone with the mark tries to cross the bridge," Nick said. "I saw with my own eyes how it catches fire. I can't explain it scientifically."

"You're going to have to suspend your scientific inclinations a lot more to understand what Westbrook is all about. The Overseer *is* the curse. He was a man at one time—a Black man."

"A Black man was in charge of supervising other Black slaves?" Nick had set down his coffee mug. He grimaced. "I've read history books about that happening, sometimes."

"The position gave him power, respect. It earned him special disposition from the master of the plantation, Robert Westbrook. A Black man eager and willing to punish, push, and chase down his own people and feed them back into the plantation's profit engine. He was a special breed indeed."

"What was his name?" Nick asked. "No one's been able to tell me his name."

"I can't tell you his name," Grandpa Lee said. "You'll have to find that out on your own. I believe he's kept that a secret for a reason. An old belief is that if you know the name of a thing, that gives you power to control it."

"He was a man, at one time," Nick said. "What happened?"

"A great fire, born of a slave insurrection." Reflections of candle flame danced in Grandpa Lee's lenses. "The Overseer was an uncommonly cruel man, even by the standards back then. From the stories I pieced together from my father, the Overseer had exacted an unusually cruel punishment on a respected family that had worked the plantation for years, for some trivial act of disobedience. It tipped the scales too far this time, and the slaves decided to revolt.

"They set the estate and most of the buildings on fire. If you've seen any of them, and I believe you have, you would recognize the signs of a conflagration—"

Nick nodded, thinking of the fire-ravaged barn and the other structures he'd seen.

"—so you can use your imagination to visualize the destruction that had torn across Westbrook at the time. Robert Westbrook and his family died in the blaze. Many others died, including some innocent. The Overseer died."

Nick frowned. "Wait, you said he was still alive?"

"I didn't say he stayed dead."

Nick bit into a thick slice of bread, chewed vigorously. He was surprised by his appetite; perhaps raw fear was like a stimulant, increasing his hunger.

"So he came back," Nick said, between bites. "Any idea how?"

"Only a theory." Grandpa took a quick sip of coffee. "I think he did so much evil in his time, shed so much innocent blood on that fertile ground, that the land itself is tainted, in a spiritual sense. I think it attracted a certain class of powerful spiritual beings—entities, you may call 'em—like flies drawn to a rotting carcass. I think the Overseer came under their influence."

"Demons," Nick said, and felt a shiver.

"That's what some people call them." Grandpa Lee chewed on a small piece of bread, swallowed. "It's why his mark has power. It comes from the land, from the spirits that have taken residence there. The land calls to people passing by. And the Overseer takes them, and the land feeds off their misery and suffering."

"You said I'd need to kill him, but you didn't say how," Nick said.

Grunting, Grandpa Lee pushed away from the table. He shuffled across the room, to his bookcase, withdrew a slim volume from the shelf, and returned to the table, placing the book in front of Nick.

Nick wiped his hands on his jeans and picked it up.

"Drawings," Nick said, turning pages. Each page held a skillfully rendered sketch of a different item, building, or place: a barn—which Nick recognized as the very barn in which he'd been imprisoned—and rooms inside the mansion, drawn with the flair of an architect.

"I've dreamed of those places, over the years," Grandpa Lee said. "I'd draw what I could remember from my dreams. I've never set foot inside the house, son." He tapped his head with his index finger. "It all came from up here."

At the back of the book, Nick found a map of the entire property.

"You've got an entire map in here," Nick said. "From what I've seen, it looks accurate, too."

"Have you ever dreamed of Westbrook?" Grandpa Lee asked. "Have you ever dreamed of him?"

Nick paused. "Today, I did, when I was locked up in the barn. I dreamed he was going to put the mark on me."

"Thirty-five years ago, after my daddy passed, I started dreaming of Westbrook and I couldn't get it out of my head." Grandpa Lee settled back into his chair. "I figured out that's how the land calls us home. It's in our blood, yours and mine. It's the burden we bear."

"The burden we bear for *what*? What did *our* ancestors do, exactly, that has put this weight on us? I don't understand our role in any of this."

But Grandpa Lee was gazing out the window, eyes clouded with worry. "It's time for you to get going, son. We could talk about this all night, but it's not going to make sense until you see it for yourself."

"Grandpa . . ." Nick shook his head, frustrated. "I don't know how to stop this guy. If I can't do that, I can't help those people get away. I can't get back my girlfriend. I need *answers*."

But his grandfather was beckoning him to the door.

"You can take my book, the shotgun, and a pocketful of shells," Grandpa Lee said. "Some water, too. That's all I can give you. You need to hurry up and get out of here."

33

Grandpa Lee wouldn't allow Nick to drive his Range Rover back into Westbrook. He said it would attract attention, and Nick reluctantly agreed with him. Nick wasn't the Caretaker, he was only the Caretaker's grandson, and as he'd seen earlier, the authorities at Westbrook who knew this about Nick considered him a potential captive like everyone else.

He had to go back into the territory on foot, on his own. Grandpa Lee remained behind at the house. Nick worried about his granddad's health, despite his apparent recovery. He worried that when he returned, he'd discover his grandfather unconscious again— or worse.

He had to put such thoughts out of mind and focus on the work ahead of him. Finding Amiya. Somehow, getting to the bottom of this Overseer business.

He jogged along the narrow dirt lane. The bridge into Westbrook proper loomed ahead, and he didn't see Raven waiting where he'd left her. He'd been gone for over an hour, he estimated. To stay safe, she would have needed to keep moving. He expected to find her at their agreed-upon rendezvous point.

He crossed the bridge, his feet thumping across the wooden planks, and reached the other side. He hurried along the road.

Gunfire rang out, dangerously loud and close. Birds, startled by the noise, took flight from the trees.

Instinctively, Nick ducked and dashed to an elm tree for cover. He crouched in the tall weeds.

His ears were ringing from the report of the gun. It had sounded like a rifle.

Clutching the pump-action shotgun his grandfather had given him, he scanned the area from which he thought the gunfire had originated. About fifty feet away, he estimated. But the problem with the foliage was that it concealed damn near everything.

Keeping to the trees and undergrowth, he advanced. He had drunk almost a gallon of water back at his granddad's house, and already his lips were dry as sandpaper. The oppressive heat wrung sweat from his pores.

Someone screamed. A woman's scream, close.

Raven, he thought.

He ran then, heedless of the risk to himself. His legs tore through vines, and he broke through screens of branches and brambles.

A man yelled, angry, and he heard sounds of struggle. Nick burst into a clearing and found them: the helper known as Jimmy had pinned Raven to the ground. He was struggling to shackle her in chains, but she was twisting and writhing like a centipede.

"Get off her!" Nick roared. Running forward, he swung the butt of the shotgun at the man's head. The meat of it connected squarely with his face. He fell backward into the grass with a grunt.

Raven scrambled away, to Nick's side. She tugged at his arm.

"We've gotta go!" she said.

But Nick didn't budge. He aimed the shotgun at Jimmy.

"Looks like I found two of y'all runaways," Jimmy said. He sat up, blinking. Blood gushed from his nose, but he seemed unconcerned. "Ain't nothin' like a two-bagger."

"You make a move and I'll shoot," Nick said. He slid his finger to the trigger.

Jimmy had a firearm, too—the rifle he had confiscated from Nick earlier. But he made no attempt to wield it. He rose to his feet. He grinned, showing a mouthful of dark, rotting teeth.

"I'm warning you, stay back," Nick said.

"You won't do nothin'," he said.

He charged Nick. In his disbelief at the man's bravado, Nick hesitated for a heartbeat, and that was all the opportunity the guy needed to invade his space. He threw a punch at Nick, his long arms granting enormous reach, and a big fist connected with Nick's midsection. It was like an explosion going off in Nick's stomach.

Purely by reflex, Nick squeezed the trigger. It probably saved his life. Buckshot sprayed from the shotgun and ripped through Jimmy's neck. The guy staggered, hit a tree, and toppled over to the ground. Blood gurgled in his ruined throat.

Nick felt sick, in more ways than one. He dropped the gun and sank to his knees, hand caressing his throbbing abdomen. A wave of nausea overcame him, and he vomited in the dirt.

Raven put a steadying hand on his shoulder. "Are you okay?"

Nodding, he drew in slow breaths. He noticed wetness on her dress.

"Did he hurt you?" he asked.

"He grazed me with a bullet, I guess." She shrugged. "I'll be okay."

"I didn't mean to kill that guy," Nick said.

He looked up and noticed Jimmy was still breathing slow, shallow breaths.

"You didn't," Raven said. "But you should have."

She picked up the shotgun.

"Hey, what are you doing?" Nick asked. He was in too much pain to get up and stop her.

Raven strolled over to the man, pumped the shotgun, and blasted him in the chest. Jimmy went still and silent. Raven studied his dead body as if he were a bug she had scraped off the sole of her shoe.

Nick didn't know what to say. Raven glanced at Nick, a challenge in her gaze, as if she dared Nick to disagree with what she'd done.

"He was the one who put the chains on me the first time," she said. "If it weren't for him, I wouldn't be stuck here."

34

They agreed to leave the helper's body where he'd fallen. It bothered Nick, though Raven assured him that the abundant scavengers in the forest would consume the corpse in due time. Nick knew all those things, of course, but the barbarity of it all disturbed him.

He hadn't been in a physical altercation, of any kind, since third grade. He didn't grow up on the streets, battling it out with local hoods and packing guns whenever he walked out his front door. He was raised in the suburbs, went to private school, and lived a sheltered, meticulously planned life.

But out here in the woods, it was survival of the fittest, and he had barely survived his first true test. Raven was only a teenager, but she was better acclimated to this place than he was, and he was fortunate to have her help.

She left the shotgun with Nick, while she took the rifle that was strapped to the helper's dead body.

"That's my granddad's rifle," Nick said. "I was going to tell you, I talked to him."

"I was about to ask why you didn't bring back help," she said. "That's what you left for, wasn't it?"

"It's not that straightforward," Nick said. "If I brought the cops in here and they tried to take all of you away, the mark on you—"

"We'd all die," Raven finished for him. "Up in smoke."

"Yeah." He shrugged. "Grandpa Lee says there's only one way to free everyone. We have to kill the Overseer."

"Well, there's a plan that no one ever thought of." Strapping the rifle over her slight frame, she marched through the woods. "Kill the Overseer—why didn't anyone else ever think of that?"

"Hey." Nick caught up to her, pain stitching his gut as he ran. That punch he'd taken to his stomach was going to hurt like hell for days. "I get the sarcasm, all right? But that's what he told me, and I know it's the truth. So do you. The Overseer, whoever he is, is the one driving Westbrook. He brought down the curse on this place— he's like the living embodiment of the curse."

"You couldn't kill that man back there on your own," Raven said. Her lips curled in derision. "You haven't seen the Overseer before. You have no idea what you're talking about doing."

"Maybe not," he said. "But that's what we've got to do. I want to get my girlfriend out of the mansion and then kill the Overseer."

"Stupid plan." Raven knocked back a branch with the rifle. "We can try to get her out—I'll help you with that. But I'm not messing with the Overseer."

"If you were going to kill the Overseer, how would you do it?" he asked.

"It's a waste of time talking about it," she said.

"Please, indulge me."

She stopped walking. She checked the sky, and looked at him.

"I'd set him on fire—and make him burn until he was nothing but ash." She brushed her fingers against the mark on her forehead. "It's exactly what he deserves for what he's done to us."

35

After Amiya finished her bath, Miss Lula took her to a musty bedroom and ordered her to get dressed.

The woman was civil toward her again. It was as if the violent incident at the bathtub was forgotten. But Amiya had learned her lesson and was keen to avoid doing anything that would provoke Miss Lula's anger. She would behave submissively, follow the woman's instructions to the letter, and stay on the alert for an opportunity to further her objective.

The bedroom was a wreck. Cobwebs wreathed the walls like curtains, and the two windows were boarded up. Old, sagging furniture—a chair, a dresser with a mirror—stood inside. A king-size, four-poster bed occupied the middle of the room.

The bed had been outfitted with fresh sheets. Amiya was tempted to lie down, but Miss Lula had other plans in store for her.

"You'll put on that dress." Miss Lula indicated a flowing, satiny red gown that hung on a hook next to the mirror. "The shoes, too."

Amiya noticed a pair of black pumps standing on the floor, beside where the dress hung, and she wanted to groan. If those shoes didn't fit, her misery quotient was going to skyrocket.

"Are those my size?" Amiya asked.

"They're close enough," Miss Lula said. Miss Lula opened one of the drawers—it opened with a harsh squeak—and removed a girdle and undergarments. "You're close in size to the master's last mistress."

Dread stirred in Amiya's chest.

"What happened to the last mistress?" Amiya asked.

"She was disobedient," Miss Lula said. Her eyes gleamed. "He turned her over to the Overseer for punishment. We never saw her again."

Amiya shuddered. Miss Lula shuffled to the doorway, putting her back toward Amiya.

"Go on and get dressed, lady."

Fortunately, the clothing fit reasonably well, including the shoes, and all of the clothes were clean, smelling of a pleasant soap. On the dresser, Amiya noticed a comb, brush, and faded containers of makeup, all of the items clustered at the base of a dusty oval mirror. Leaning forward, she rubbed clean a spot on the glass with the heel of her hand. She picked up the brush and stared at her reflection.

All dressed up and nowhere to go . . .

A sob swelled in her throat. She tried to choke it down, but it burst out of her, rocked her like an earthquake tremor, bringing forth scalding hot tears that slid down her face and spattered on the top of the dresser.

I can't do this. I can't pretend that I'm accepting this life. This is ridiculous! I won't—

"Get it together, lady!" Miss Lula said from the doorway. "Crying's not gonna change a thing."

It was a reprimand that her mother had often lobbed at her when Amiya was a young girl, and the familiarity of it had the odd effect of calming Amiya's abraded nerves. Her mother had despised tears, though she had no compunctions about letting them flow in abundance whenever it suited her manipulative aims. If Amiya had ever wanted to cry, she had to do so in secret.

It would be the same here in Westbrook, she realized.

Amiya sniffled, sucked in a shaky breath. She found a silk hand-kerchief tucked on the corner of the dresser. She used it to blot her eyes and dry her nose.

As best she could, she brushed her damp hair. She thought of asking Miss Lula if they had a blow dryer but doubted the woman would have found her little joke amusing.

The makeup kit was old, but she was able to work with it. She applied blush and a small amount of the ruby-red lipstick.

"Put on that perfume, too," Miss Lula said. "It's the master's favorite."

Amiya picked up the glass bottle of what looked like an old French perfume, based on the faded letters on the front. It had a sweet, woodsy odor.

"When do I get to meet the master?" Amiya asked.

"Soon as it's dark," Miss Lula said. "He likes to have some alone time with a new mistress before she gets marked, to get acquainted."

He sounds like a swell guy, Amiya thought, and had to suppress a giggle. *How gentlemanly of him to want to meet before I get branded like a prize steer.*

"Where is the master now?" Amiya asked.

"You said you were hungry. Do you want me to stand here answering questions that will answer themselves in time, or do you want to eat?"

Chastened, Amiya applied perfume to both of her wrists and dabbed a bit on her neck. The only time she really wore fragrance these days was when she was going out with Nick. Thinking about Nick, wondering when she would see him again, provoked another tremor at the base of her throat, and she had to set those thoughts aside.

She checked herself in the mirror one final time, liked what she saw, and approached Miss Lula at the doorway.

"Ready," Amiya said.

Miss Lula assessed her from head to toe. Amiya caught a brief sparkle of desire in her eyes, but Miss Lula quickly looked away and gave only a curt nod.

She would not fool the woman again.

She followed Miss Lula downstairs. Navigating the damaged hardwood floor in heels was like walking a tightrope. While going down the staircase, she nearly lost her balance, and Miss Lula grabbed her arm and scooped her upright.

"You'll get used to it," Miss Lula said.

On the first floor, she guided Amiya into the dining room. It was a large chamber, dominated by a long, round table that could have accommodated a party of twenty, and surrounded by chairs carved of mahogany. A white tablecloth, tattered and browned at the edges, covered the surface, topped by a cracked vase from which bristled fresh petunias. A chandelier wearing a garland of cobwebs swung from a chain above the center of the table. Candles flickered on a pair of side tables.

No one was in the room, but Amiya heard the rattle and clatter of staff—*not staff, prisoners,* she reminded herself—working in the kitchen beyond a set of closed double doors. The air smelled of warm, delicious things.

Miss Lula pulled out a chair at the head of the table. "Sit, lady."

"I feel as if I'm in the dining room at the Ritz-Carlton," Amiya said.

Miss Lula's gaze was dull, reflecting no recognition of what Amiya had said. *How long has this woman been here?*

Long enough to have no idea that the Ritz was a popular chain of luxury hotels, most likely, and Amiya found that deeply disturbing.

She settled onto the chair. Miss Lula put her hand on her shoulder and gave Amiya a squeeze that sent a hot current of pain down Amiya's arm.

"Ouch, that hurts," Amiya said.

"You'll wait in here, lady, in this chair." Miss Lula gave her a stern look. "I'll go ask the staff to bring you some food."

"I'm not going anywhere, Miss Lula, I promise." *For now*, she thought.

Miss Lula nodded, took her hand off Amiya's shoulder. While Amiya massaged her muscle where the woman had squeezed her, Miss Lula left the room via the double doors that led to the kitchen.

Amiya's gaze tracked to the other doorway. It was ten feet to the entry hall. Perhaps another twenty feet to the front door. She could outrun the big, lumbering Miss Lula, probably even while wearing a pair of heels.

But there were others in the house, too, people she had not yet met. They might attempt to stop her. At this point, Amiya didn't have a single ally who might help her escape.

He turned her over to the Overseer for punishment. We never saw her again.

She couldn't afford to launch an ill-considered escape plan. The penalty for failure was too severe. She had to bide her time.

But she had to get out of here before they marked her. Instinctively, she understood that she had to avoid the brand, at all costs. The effect of the symbol on these captives might have been only psychological, but it was powerful. Despite all her learnings, she wasn't immune to the effects of such things: she could find herself living here like everyone else, with no hope of ever getting out, without so much as a memory of her life before.

I will not let that happen.

Across the dining room, the double doors swung open.

A slender, handsome young Black man entered, carrying a large white soup bowl from which fragrant steam rose. He wore tattered dark slacks and a white dress shirt with a faded maroon tie, his sleeves rolled up at the elbows.

His head was bald, which gave her a clear look at the "W" branded on his forehead.

"Good afternoon, lady," he said, and smiled at her. His eyes were shy, but kind. "I brought you chicken soup."

"Thank you." She sat up straighter in the chair. "I'm Amiya. What's your name?"

"Ossie." He set down the bowl in front of her, unfolded a white napkin and a set of silverware: spoon, fork, and a knife sharp enough to slice a steak.

"Oh, like Ossie Davis," she said, studiously avoiding staring at the knife. "The actor."

"Uh, yeah." He looked away from her.

She glanced into the bowl, saw chunks of chicken and vegetables swimming in broth. Her stomach ached with hunger.

"This looks delicious," she said. "Are you one of the cooks here?"

"One of them, yeah." He fidgeted with his tie and wouldn't meet her gaze. "Oh, I'll go get you some water. Be right back."

The dress she wore had a small front pocket. Amiya slipped the knife inside, reassured by its coldness against her thigh. Whether Ossie had brought it to her by accident, she couldn't be sure, but she was keen to take advantage of any opportunity to arm herself.

Amiya spread the napkin across her nap and examined the spoon. It was silver, and clean. The mansion might have been falling apart, but someone was washing dishes.

She took a sip of the soup. It was hot and tasty, and she had to check herself from lifting up the bowl in both hands and slurping it down like a beggar in a back alley.

Ossie returned with a glass pitcher full of water, and a tall glass.

"The soup is wonderful," she said. "I really mean that. Thank you for bringing it to me. I was famished."

"Okay." He poured her a glass of water. He stood at attention beside the table as if he were her personal server. "The lady gets the best."

"Other than working in the kitchen, what else do you do here?" Amiya asked. She sipped her soup.

"Whatever needs to be done," Ossie said. "There's always something to do." He cast a sidelong glance toward the kitchen, a hint of anxiety glimmering in his eyes. "Miss Lula keeps us real busy."

He doesn't want to be here either, Amiya thought. She placed his age in the mid-twenties. He should have been finishing up college and embarking on a career doing something worthwhile, not bringing her soup and working in a house that needed to be flattened by a wrecking ball.

But after the debacle in the bathtub with Miss Lula, Amiya had resolved to be more careful. She didn't know whom she could trust.

Still, this young man might prove to be an ally.

36

"I'm bringing you here only because we still have daylight," Raven said. She peeled aside a veil of branches with the barrel of the rifle. She motioned Nick forward. "But there it is. Go look if you want."

She had taken him to the edge of the plantation. In the distance, he could see the master's mansion and other buildings, but the residence to which she had brought him interested Nick most of all.

He shouldered past her and peered through the trees.

It was a small log cabin. It looked the way it must have the morning after it had been set on fire. The wood was dark with soot and ash, and the door sagged in the frame. The shingles had peeled away like singed strips of skin.

"The Overseer lived here?" Nick asked.

"That's what people say." Raven shuddered, looked around warily. "At night, it looks different."

"Brand new?" Nick said.

She nodded. "I hear, he comes out of there."

"If he comes out of there at nightfall, that means he's in there *right now.*" Nick felt his heart rate pick up. He lifted his shotgun. "We can go in there and put an end to all of this."

"I'm not going in there." Raven was shaking her head. "You can go. This is as close as I get to him. This place is evil."

Her reaction didn't make any sense to him. This man that everyone here seemed to fear arriving at night happened to live by day in a ramshackle hut, and no one did anything about it? It wasn't as though the cabin was protected by a barbed wire fence and an armed sentry.

"I'm going in," Nick said.

Raven settled next to a tree, didn't make any move to follow him. Shrugging, he advanced.

As he neared the house, he questioned the idea that anyone lived here at all. He didn't hear a thing—no sounds of life issued from within. The breeze whispered through the ruined slats of wood. When he set foot on the porch, the wood groaned under his weight as if it might collapse.

His heart knocked, but he attributed that to Raven's bizarre reaction seeping into his subconscious thoughts. Her anxiety was contagious. From a logical perspective, there was nothing to fear.

There's nothing here, only a fire-damaged home.

The doorknob was black with old soot. He pulled it. The door, sagging and warped by the old fire, resisted his attempt to tug it open.

How can the Overseer come out of this damned place if I can't get in it?

He set the shotgun aside on the ground. Using both of his hands, he got a firm grip on the knob, planted his right foot on the frame, and pulled with all of his strength, his arms quaking from the strain.

Wood creaked and crackled. Encouraged, he doubled his effort. The door loosened and came open with a shriek of protesting wood.

Something flew toward him with a leathery flutter of wings. Nick ducked, shielded his head with his arms.

Bats, of course. Only bats.

The creatures funneled out of the house and darted away into the trees. Nick picked up the shotgun, glanced across the yard toward Raven.

She looked scared, arms braced over her chest as she nibbled at her bottom lip. He had to teach her, and perhaps others, that there was nothing to be afraid of here. They had lived in this backward community for so long, bound here by strange magic, that all reasonable thought had left them. It didn't have to be that way.

Gripping the shotgun, Nick edged through the doorway.

It was a one-room house, like his grandfather's, and the interior was in worse condition than the exterior. The few pieces of furniture inside—a table, a dresser with a cracked mirror, a narrow bed—had been scorched by flames. Sections of the floor had collapsed inward. Several beams had fallen from the ceiling, too. Patches of gray light came inside through the damaged roof.

There was no one inside. The only possible resting place for the man was perhaps down in the dusty blackness underneath the ruptured floor, and the notion that anyone could live in such a place was absurd.

He didn't hear any other burrowing creatures either.

Nevertheless, he ventured deeper into the home. As he moved, he was careful to avoid the weakened floorboards.

He noticed several items on the dresser that he hadn't spotted from his initial glance around. A brown felt Stetson-style hat lay atop a black pea coat. Both pieces of clothing were in good condition, as if recently worn.

"Is anyone in here?" he said, sounding silly to himself. Of course no one was in here. But he looked around again, his gaze sharp.

He was alone. Obviously.

He placed the shotgun on the edge of the dresser. He picked up the hat by its wide brim.

His fingers tingled, as if soft static electricity coursed through the material. He traced his index finger along the creased edge, energy rippling through his skin.

Don't touch it.

Dismissing the interior voice as ridiculous, Nick placed the hat on his head. He checked his profile in the mirror. The square-shaped glass was intact, not cracked as he had thought at first.

The hat was a perfect fit. It looked good on him. Most of all, it *felt* good, like putting on a favorite piece of clothing he'd owned for years.

He looked at the pea coat. It appeared to be his size. It was a warm day for April, but the evening promised to be cool. He would need the protection it offered.

He slipped on the coat. It was a perfect fit, too. He looked at himself in the mirror.

He had acquired a thick beard, as though he hadn't shaved in weeks. A scar curved along the outer edge of his left eye, a remnant of a knife attack that he'd fended off from one of the field hands.

"They need discipline," he whispered to himself. He smiled. "All of them, they lack it. I'm here to enforce the law."

His leather bull whip lay across the dresser. He gripped the handle. It was pleasingly heavy in his hands, a weapon designed to dispense brutal, well-deserved punishment.

"I've got to teach them," he said. "Pain is their friend."

A rifle cracked, and the mirror shattered, shards flying. Startled, Nick dropped the whip, spun around.

Raven was in the doorway, aiming the rifle at him.

"Take off the hat," she said, her voice like iron. "Or, I swear to God, I'll shoot you."

Nick blinked. He felt as if he had dozed off and had awakened to find this girl pointing the gun at him for no reason.

"I don't . . . I don't know what happened," he said. He touched the hat on his head and had no recollection of putting it on. He pulled it off and let it drop to the floor.

"The coat, too," Raven said.

He peeled off the coat—why he had put that on in the first place was a mystery to him—and let it sink to the floorboards.

Looking around as if something might leap from the shadows to attack her, Raven came inside.

"I warned you, this place is evil," she said. Using the rifle barrel, she nudged the hat, coat, and whip into a dark chasm in the floor. She took Nick by the arm, her fingers cold with clammy sweat.

"Get your gun and let's get out of here," she said.

37

Amiya was so hungry she could have devoured the chicken soup in three minutes flat, but she forced herself to slow down and savor each spoonful. She didn't know when she might eat again and needed to enjoy this meal.

Eating slow also gave her more time with Ossie. Miss Lula hadn't yet returned; it sounded as if she were haranguing the workers in the kitchen.

Amiya caught Ossie looking at her from the corner of his eye. She crossed her legs, took a sip of water, and in what she hoped was a casual tone, asked: "Who is Tanya?"

Ossie gave her such a look of shock that she might have tossed her glass of cold water in his face.

"How do you know about my mama?" he asked in a taut whisper. He glanced over his shoulder at the kitchen doors.

With a nod, Amiya indicated the name tattooed on Ossie's exposed forearm. "I thought it might have been your girlfriend or daughter, but to hear it's your mother, that says a lot to me about what kind of young man you are, Ossie. You cherish your mother."

It was as if she had depressed a trigger in his heart, releasing an outpouring of pent-up emotion. He came to the table and knelt next to her. Tears swam in his eyes. His breath was hot.

"Don't let him mark you," Ossie said. "You won't ever get out of here if he does."

"How do I get out before that happens?" Amiya closed her hand over his, squeezed. "Please, Ossie. I'll do whatever I can to help you, too. My boyfriend is here—they have him outside. We'll both help you, I promise."

"They're gonna make him a field hand." Ossie sneered at the term. "They said I was too pretty for a man to be working outside."

"None of us want to be here," she said. "I thought about just running out the front door."

"No." Ossie shook his head. "The helpers out there would run you down like it was nothing. They're a lot faster than they look. Stronger, too."

Amiya thought about Miss Lula, how the woman had pinned her underwater in the bathtub. A shiver passed through her.

"Things here aren't what they seem to be, you gotta know that," Ossie said. "At night, it's all different. You have to see it to believe it."

"I want to get out of here before it gets dark."

"You need to wait, 'cause you ain't gonna get past the helpers." He glanced over his shoulder again, hunched closer to her. "Listen, the master's gonna want to see you before the Overseer marks you. The master has keys on him, I've seen them, and he keeps a gun. No one can really get close to him."

"But I could." Her heart knocked, and she felt dizzy at the prospect of what may lie ahead.

"You gotta be careful. The rumor is, the last mistress tried to take his gun, too. She's not here anymore, but I don't think that means she went home."

Amiya remembered Miss Lula's warning: *He turned her over to the Overseer for punishment. We never saw her again.*

"If I can get ahold of these keys, and the firearm, then what do I do?" she asked.

Ossie started to answer when the kitchen doors crashed open with a boom like a thunderclap.

"Get away from the lady!" Miss Lula shouted.

Amiya was so startled that she dropped her spoon, the silverware clattering into her bowl of soup. Miss Lula stormed like an enraged elephant across the dining room, feet pounding the floorboards. Ossie snapped upright and put his hands at his sides like a soldier standing at attention.

"You." Miss Lula put her long, thick finger in Ossie's face. Ossie cringed as if he expected a blow. "Pick up these dishes and get back into the kitchen."

"Yes, ma'am." Ossie nodded crisply and stepped toward the table. He avoided Amiya's gaze as he reached for her bowl.

"But I wasn't finished eating," Amiya said.

"You'll eat again later, lady," Miss Lula said. "The master always insists on a big dinner with his mistress before he takes her to his bedroom for the night." Miss Lula grinned. "He's always been such a romantic."

38

"When I put on those clothes, I was *him*," Nick said. "I looked in the mirror and saw his face, but it was my face, like I'd stepped into his skin. I had his thoughts about beating people, disciplining them. That whip in my hand felt like the most powerful weapon on the planet."

"Evil," Raven said for perhaps the fifth time. They walked shoulder to shoulder through the woods, away from the Overseer's cabin. Birds flitted through the treetops, disturbed by their advance through the forest. "I got a bad feeling when you went in there, like you were sinking into a deep hole and you'd never get out. We never should have gone there in the first place. Sorry."

"I'm glad you got me out when you did," Nick said, "but I needed to see it for myself. Don't be sorry. I feel as if I learned something important."

"Learned what?" Raven stopped, standing beside an elm tree. Her gaze probed him. "What'd you find out that's important?"

"I learned about the power of this place, this land." He swept his hand around them. "It can remake itself and make you see things that you couldn't have imagined."

"Oh, okay." She started to turn forward, stopped herself, squinted at him. She looked far, far older than her years. "That's it, then?"

"Yeah."

He was lying to her, and he believed she probably suspected his dishonesty. She was young, but she had witnessed a lot in her short life and knew how to read people, and he had never been particularly good at lying anyway. Back in college, when his group of friends played Texas Hold'em, his buddies had always been able to call his bluff.

But he was too afraid to share what he was really thinking.

Grandpa Lee says we're bound to this place. After spending time in the Overseer's cabin, wearing his clothes, slipping into his skin, dipping into his thoughts, I'm starting to figure out why—and it disturbs the hell out of me.

"Where are we going now?" Nick asked, wanting to change the subject. "We need to get Amiya out of the house."

"We can't stroll up to the front door and ask her to come out," Raven said. She laughed, a bitter sound. "They've got helpers walking around outside, usually two or three. We took down Jimmy but we got lucky. They're already looking for us, too. Then—"

"Then what?"

"Then, if we get into the house, we gotta deal with Miss Lula." Raven let out a deep sigh, kicked a broken branch at her feet. "That's not a fight we can win."

"But both of us have guns," Nick said. "A rifle and a shotgun."

"I don't know if a gun would hurt her," Raven said. "I know it sounds crazy, but I used to work in the kitchen in Westbrook. I saw Miss Lula take a cake out of the oven with her bare hands and it didn't bother her one bit. She's a helper, but it's like she's more than they are, too."

"Like an uber helper," he said.

"Something like that, yeah. She's the most respected out of all of them. They seem scared of her, too."

Nick couldn't help but worry about how Amiya was coping in such circumstances. He loved her, but she had an uncanny knack for knowing how to push someone's buttons, and if this Miss Lula was the one in charge it was unavoidable that Amiya would have tried to work her somehow, to gain an advantage. It sounded as if doing so would have been a mistake.

Amiya, I'm sorry for bringing you here. All of this is my fault.

Nick decided that if he ever saw Amiya again—*when* he saw her again, he chastened himself—he would come clean on everything with her. The money they owed to Shango, his plan to persuade Grandpa Lee to sell the property so he could pay him off, the whole sordid tale. She would be angry and might even leave him for good. He wouldn't blame her if she did.

But first he had to get her out of Westbrook.

"I agree that we can't knock on the front door and demand that they send Amiya outside," Nick said. "That would be suicide. What else did you have in mind?"

"I had help when I escaped," Raven said. "We had gotten some keys, but that wasn't enough. We still had to slip out without anyone noticing."

"You created a diversion," Nick said.

"Right." Raven smiled a little. "It was my idea. I put something in the oven that blew up. When Miss Lula and another helper were checking that out, we made our move. No one tried to stop us."

"Clever girl," Nick said. "If it worked once, why not do it again?"

39

Daylight was slipping away, the sun fading like a dying ember. Nick estimated that full sunset was less than an hour away.

But their plan demanded stealth, and patience.

Skirting the plantation's perimeter by staying hidden in the surrounding undergrowth, they had neared a large clapboard structure that Raven informed him served as Westbrook's warehouse. Household goods, farm equipment, straw, and countless other essential items were kept inside those soot-colored walls behind a set of wide, locked double doors, under the watchful eye of a helper who could have been a stunt double for the Incredible Hulk.

"That guy is huge," Nick said in a low voice. He knelt beside a tree, foliage camouflaging his head. They had a view of the storehouse from the eastward side, the building about twenty yards away from where they had taken cover.

The guard wore a soiled brown shirt, tattered jeans, and work boots. He sat on the short, wobbly-looking staircase that led to the warehouse doors. He fiddled with a long, broad length of wood that he kept across his lap.

"Huge but dumb," Raven whispered. "Slow, too. They call him Tank. Tank's able to scare away anyone who might think of stealing something from inside, 'cause of how he looks. He's really strong, too. If he got his hands on us, we're dead."

"We won't let that happen," Nick said. He glanced at his watch. "Does he ever take a break or anything?"

"He'll go to use the outhouse nearby every few hours. He only does that when someone else comes to stand watch while he's gone. A different helper takes over at night, too, but we can't wait that long."

"We've got to draw him away from the doors," Nick said.

Without a word of warning, Raven took a small rock out of her pocket and flung it. The stone sailed across the grass and landed at Tank's feet.

Nick glared at Raven. "What the hell are you doing—are you nuts?"

But the girl only grinned at him, and started scrambling through the undergrowth, keeping low to the ground.

Tank was on his feet. He swept his gaze across the woods, the wood levered like a baseball bat over his shoulder.

Cursing, Nick duck-walked after Raven. His knees popped. Bushes scraped across his sweaty face. The kid was so fast that he struggled to keep up with her.

She's going to get us killed out here, he thought.

But she had spunk in spades. Giggling, she popped up like a mole and flung another stone toward Tank.

The rock bounced off the big man's shoulder. He stomped toward the trees, dust pluming from his large feet. He seemed unclear on where to look, however, grimacing as he surveyed the area, and he went toward the section that Nick and Raven had left over a minute ago.

Nick wiped perspiration out of his eyes and hustled after Raven. She moved like black lightning through the woods, circling around the perimeter of the warehouse. Occasionally she popped up and peppered Tank with a stone, and the distraction always sent him in the wrong direction, keeping him a good distance behind their true location.

When they had reached the other side of the building, Raven broke cover and dashed to the doors. Nick ran after her.

"You're insane," he said.

"It worked, didn't it?"

She had her keys out already. The doors were secured by a heavy padlock slipped through a hasp. She jabbed a key into the padlock's slot, and twisted.

The lock disengaged with a click. Nick pocketed the lock and helped her to heave the doors open. They whispered open on oiled hinges.

The warehouse beckoned, dense with shadow. Nick squinted and made out aisle after aisle of different items, stacked on pallets that lay on a floor coated in sawdust.

"Hurry in before he comes back this way," Raven said.

She needn't have said anything. Nick ran inside so fast he nearly stumbled over his own feet. Together, they pulled the doors shut, blotting out the daylight.

"Do you think he'll notice the padlock is gone?" Nick asked. "I didn't want to risk getting locked in here."

"He's not very bright," she said. "I doubt it."

They backed away from the doors. Gray light filtered into the building from several windows set high above the floor, but mostly shadows dominated the space.

Nick stepped to the nearest row of products. They were bags of flour, with old-fashioned labels of brands he didn't recognize.

"This stuff is old," he said. "Do they ever restock it with anything new?"

"They never run out of supplies," Raven said. "The building restocks itself every night."

He stared at her. "Restocks itself?"

"If you were to take out that bag of flour right next to you"—she pointed—"when you came back in here tomorrow, it would be there again, like you'd never touched it."

"You've seen this happen?"

She nodded. "Miss Lula would send me in here all the time to get different things for the kitchen. You need matches, right?"

"Yeah." He couldn't wrap his mind around what she had shared with him, but he decided that it didn't matter. The only way he could operate in this fantastical new reality was to roll with the punches as they came. "Matches. Paper. Candles. Glue. I highly doubt we'll find flash powder in here so we'll have to sacrifice a couple of shotgun shells for their gunpowder."

"I've never seen anyone make homemade firecrackers," she said.

"When I was working on my doctorate, some of us students did it for fun," he said. "Our summer project was to create a Fourth of July fireworks show using products we created ourselves."

"That sounds kinda dangerous."

"It was. Dangerous and stupid—it's amazing no one got hurt. But I learned quite a bit." He had to smile. "I never thought any of it would turn out actually to be useful."

Raven scurried from one aisle to the next, collecting items like a squirrel gathering nuts, Nick following close behind. Once she had located matches and a box of white taper candles, Nick lit one of them and used its flickering light to guide their search, holding it aloft like a tomb raider bearing a torch.

They took all the ingredients to a small oak desk at the back of the warehouse. A leather-bound ledger lay on the desktop. Nick cracked open the book and saw barely legible, handwritten entries on the crisp white pages.

"This is where they tracked inventory," he said. "This place is like a living museum."

"It's the same inside the house," Raven said. "They spend all day cleaning and washing and stuff, but then everything's back to how it was before the next morning. Like that old Greek myth guy, Sisyphus, pushing the boulder up the hill only to see it roll back down."

"You're a reader, huh?" he said, impressed.

"It's not like we got TV and Wi-Fi here." She cleared space on the desk and sorted out the items they had collected. "Okay, Mr. Science Wiz, do your thing."

A sudden booming noise made Nick flinch. Raven's eyes flashed with alarm. She looked over her shoulder, then spun back to Nick, her face pinched with fear.

"Sounds like Tank isn't as dumb as we thought," Nick said.

40

Nick blew out his candle, shadows rising to surround them like a gathering of old friends. Raven went to grab her rifle, but Nick put his hand on her arm and shook his head.

"We shoot at him in here and the gunshot will echo and alert every helper at Westbrook." He had dropped his voice to a whisper. "We'd be trapped."

She grimaced as the realization settled over her, lowered the weapon. She whispered: "What you wanna do?"

"Get out of here before he finds us." He motioned behind her. "We can empty one of those sacks of rice over there and store our things in it. I'll have to put together our toys somewhere else."

They heard heavy footsteps shuffling across the sawdust-covered floor. It sounded as if the helper was methodically searching the warehouse, square foot by square foot.

Nope, he's not dumb by a long shot, Nick thought. Circles of cold sweat had formed in his armpits.

Raven helped him pick up a sack of rice; it must have weighed at least fifty pounds. He tore open the tough material with the utility tool Grandpa Lee had given him. Together, they dumped the rice in a spot on the corner of the floor, letting the grains quietly pool into a pile.

"All right, let's hurry." He swept everything off the table and into the empty sack. He didn't have anything to tie it closed, so he used his leather belt.

Near the middle of the warehouse, something clanged to the floor. The big man muttered under his breath.

He had gotten much closer to them.

Nick picked up the shotgun off the desk. Pulling the trigger in there would be suicide but he felt safer with the steel in his hands. Raven hefted the rifle, too.

Tank was drawing closer, feet clopping across the floor. Nick hefted the bag of their items over his shoulder, using the belt as a carrying strap.

"This way," Raven said, and pointed to their left. "We can slip around him."

The girl had proven adept at sneaking around. He followed her lead without question. She guided him to the end of the row, where they took cover behind a stack of wooden pallets.

Nick paused, listening. It sounded as if Tank was to their right, and behind them. He nudged Raven, and they continued forward, traveling through alternating patches of shadow and darkening light. Their footsteps were silent, the sounds of their passage masked by the thin layer of sawdust blanketing the floor. But Nick's heart was booming like a bass drum in his chest.

As Nick edged forward across another aisle, his shoulder brushed past something that came loose. He turned to catch it, but too late.

A glass tumbled away and broke against the floor.

A few aisles over, Tank grunted with interest. His footsteps quickened their pace.

Nick and Raven didn't hesitate. They kept moving, cutting a right into the next aisle. Deep shadows dwelled in that area. Nick squinted to make out what lay ahead of him.

Raven fell over a low, dark shape that blocked the aisle. Some kind of crate. She stifled a short cry, but Nick heard their pursuer chuckle.

He had them running scared, and he knew it.

Nick groped for Raven's thin arm, grabbed her, and pulled her upright. They ran down the aisle then, knocking past boxes and other packaged sundries, their feet kicking up a storm of sawdust. Stealth didn't matter anymore. They needed only to get to the doorway.

"Right, go right," Raven whispered, out of breath.

Nick whirled in the direction she gave him—and ran into a solid wall of pure muscle. He staggered backward a couple of steps, fought to get his bearings.

Tank grunted. He stepped forward into a shaft of daylight.

Outside of working on this nightmarish plantation, Nick thought the guy could have been a defensive tackle on an NFL team. He was easily six-foot-six, over three hundred pounds. This close to him, Nick found his sheer size so intimidating that he felt something in him wilt.

It's over—we're not getting past him.

"Y'all ain't supposed to be in here," Tank said, in a voice that rumbled like thunder. "Come on back with me to the house and we gonna talk to Miss Lula."

"Miss Lula sent us in here to get some rice," Raven said.

"You the runaway," Tank said, pointing at her. "I ain't fooled." He shifted his thick index finger to Nick. "You new here—they told me 'bout you. You ain't got the mark yet."

Nick swung the shotgun toward Tank. It was already chambered with a shell.

"Step aside, please," Nick said. "I don't want to pull the trigger, but I will if you don't get out of our way."

At this, Tank only smiled.

"Go 'head," he said.

As recently as this morning, Nick was a man who abhorred

violence. When he saw news stories on TV of violent confrontations that ended in death and misery, he tended to think: *Why did that have to happen? Was that really the only way these people could have found a resolution?* He was a gun owner but never thought he'd point a firearm at anyone. Owning such a powerful weapon was the equivalent of insurance in the event of some extreme circumstance.

He realized that he had arrived at the knife's edge of extreme circumstances, and he was surprised by the swiftness of his reaction.

He leveled the shotgun at Tank and shot the man in the stomach.

The Mossberg boomed like a cannon in the enclosed space, the windows trembling in their frames, and the recoil snapped through Nick's wrists.

Grimacing, Tank sank to his knees. Blood peppered his abdomen. But he didn't go down. Any other man, shot at point-blank range with a twelve-gauge shotgun, would have been flattened like a pancake.

"Let's go!" Raven said.

Tank roared, face contorted in concentration like a powerlifter performing a dead lift. As if he were absorbing the pain, pushing his body through the agony.

Raven pushed Nick. Nick broke into a run.

He looked over his shoulder. Behind them, Tank was getting to his feet again.

It was yet another incredible incident in a growing collection of improbabilities, and if Nick survived this ordeal, he knew he would never view the world the same way again.

Raven bolted ahead of him, to the doorway. The doors had been pulled shut, for which Nick thought they might be grateful. It might have muffled the sound of the shotgun.

They strained to pull the heavy doors open. Nick heard Tank coming, the man's furious footsteps increasing in speed.

They hustled through the doorway, into the darkening day. Nick slammed the hasp into place, dug into his pocket, and fumbled out the padlock.

He slipped the lock into the hasp just as Tank rammed against the doors like a caged bull. The doors buckled, wood groaning. The lock rattled, but held. Hands shaking, Nick engaged the padlock.

Roaring, Tank slammed against the doors again.

"All that noise is going to draw someone out here soon," Raven said, looking around them. "We better get somewhere safe."

41

S tuck in the same bedroom where she had dressed earlier, Amiya watched out the cracked second-floor window as the last rays of sunshine bled out of the day.

All dressed up and nowhere to go, she thought. She put her fist to her mouth to suppress a manic giggle.

She had heard so much about what would happen next—the master would see her at dinner; the master would "romance" her before taking her to his chamber; the plantation itself transformed radically at nightfall; the Overseer would mark her only after her date with the master—but she hadn't a clue about what might actually happen. It was as if everyone there were privy to some great secret, excluding her.

She was still inclined to believe that every one of them had been systematically programmed and were living under a mass delusion. All of them were truly captives. Some of them, such as Miss Lula, had been there so long they no longer desired to leave. Others, such as her new ally, Ossie, still had enough of a connection to his former life to want to escape.

She wanted to help Ossie and anyone else trustworthy who

wanted to come with her, but first, she needed to help herself. Her number one priority was safely getting out of the house.

Miss Lula had brought her to the bedroom and left Amiya there, unattended, as if she no longer considered her a threat.

"You'll wait here until I come to collect you later," Miss Lula had said. She had shut the door behind her, but it didn't sound as if she had locked it.

Amiya still had the steak knife she had stolen from the dining room. It wouldn't be enough to take down Miss Lula—that woman looked strong enough to sustain a point-blank blast from a cannon—but used at the right moment, it could give her an advantage.

Amiya tested the doorknob. The brass was scorched, but it yielded to her hand. She pulled the door open, tensed, expecting Miss Lula to be waiting on the other side ready to yell at her, but the woman was out of sight. The corridor was empty, lit only by a single wavering candle.

Ossie had warned her against an escape attempt, had cautioned her to bide her time until she encountered the master. She was inclined to accept his advice, yet she needed a better understanding of her environment.

She slipped off the high heels and left them inside the bedroom. Barefoot, she stepped into the hallway, the dark wood cool underneath her soles, the dress sweeping around her legs.

The mansion was as large as a boutique hotel. Once, she had traveled with her family to Paris and they had lodged in an establishment in the Le Marais historic district. The wide hardwood corridors, high-ceilinged rooms, crown molding, and general air of tainted decadence reminded her of that place, which, thanks to her mother, had been one of the worst vacations of her life.

The room in which she had been placed was near the midpoint of the hallway. The canted spiral staircase stood slightly ahead; it twisted ever upward, leading to an even higher floor of the estate. The balustrade looked ready to collapse, the wood half-eaten by flames. Weak light filtered to the stairs, possibly from a skylight.

She padded to the foot of the steps and peered upward. She saw only patches of light and shadow. The fading light came in through a damaged section of the ceiling up there.

She glanced over the railing at the spiral beneath her, saw no one watching. Lips pressed together, she took to the ascending section of the staircase, taking care to avoid the warped steps and the debris left behind from the old fire.

On the third floor, the air was thick and warm, and immediately wrung perspiration from her pores. The landing emptied into a wide open space, which brought to mind a spacious loft. Part of the ceiling had collapsed, boards buckled as if warped out of shape by giant hands. Several windows, old but intact, were spaced throughout the chamber.

Across the room, someone was staring out one of those windows.

It looked like an elderly woman. She wore a tattered white house-dress, and her gray hair fanned across her narrow shoulders. She was perched at the window like a child gazing outdoors waiting on a beloved parent to arrive.

"This is my favorite part of the day," the woman said, in a brittle voice that crackled with excitement. Without looking over her shoulder at Amiya, she waved her over with a liver-spotted hand. "Come lookie, dear."

She punctuated her invitation with a giggle. The sound of her laughter raised the hackles at the back of Amiya's neck. Instead of approaching her, Amiya stepped to a nearby window that faced the same direction.

From her vantage point, Amiya could see the front of Westbrook, twilight settling over the plantation: the fields, the various buildings that supported the operation. She noticed that the field hands had vanished; off work, perhaps?

She could see the barn in which they had imprisoned Nick, a boxy shape in the gathering gloom. Her heart clutched. Was he still in there?

"Here it comes!" the woman cried. She was suddenly beside

Amiya, one gnarled hand clutching Amiya's shoulder with frenzied strength. She pointed out the window.

Amiya started to push the woman away but stopped when she saw the thing the woman had indicated. She stared, lips parted.

For a moment, her heart stopped.

A towering wave of darkness rolled across the land, like an apocalyptic tsunami. But this was a wall of blackness, not water. It was coming directly for them, rippling across the plantation as swiftly as the wind.

Amiya squeezed her eyes shut, a scream trapped at the base of her throat.

Coldness tore through her, bone deep, as if she had been flash frozen. It felt like a million icy pinpricks on her skin. The pain was so intense that she thought she might pass out.

As quickly as it came, it was over.

Shuddering, she opened her eyes. Closed them, opened them again.

Laughing, arms spread wide, the old woman raced to the staircase with the giddiness of a child on Christmas morning. Her dress, previously soiled and tattered, fluttered around her, fresh and new.

The staircase glistened richly, too, as if recently restored.

Amiya put her hand to her mouth. Heart pounding, she turned, taking in the loft.

This can't be, she thought, gazing at the perfectly formed ceiling, the shining hardwoods, the sparkling windows. *This place had been falling apart.*

Not trusting her balance, she shuffled to the head of the staircase. She put her hand on the balustrade. The mahogany, in pristine condition, was cool underneath her fingers.

It felt real. Indisputably.

Piano music had struck up from somewhere downstairs. She recognized the rich, sonorous notes of "Moonlight Sonata," and she remembered the crumbling grand piano she had seen in the parlor.

A spell of dizziness spun through her. She grasped the balustrade to assist her balance, simultaneously realizing that she was holding onto something that shouldn't have existed in its current condition.

Laughter bubbled up from the lower levels, too. She heard chattering, excited voices. The clink and clatter of glasses.

It's like a party has started, she thought.

Although she feared what she might see, worried that whatever she would discover would blow away her sanity for good, she descended the staircase to the second level.

Candlelight brightened the corridor. The hallway had been restored to a state of grandeur.

Miss Lula emerged from the doorway of the bedroom that had been assigned to Amiya. Amiya was taken aback by the older woman's appearance. Not only was she smiling, but her clothes had been revitalized.

She even wore a string of pearls.

"There you are, lady," Miss Lula said. "Come and put on your shoes and freshen up your makeup. It's time to meet the master."

42

Nick was huddled over his batch of homemade flash-bangs when the transforming darkness swept over the land.

He hadn't known exactly what to expect. He and Raven had slipped back into the forest and found a quiet, sheltered place within a copse of elms in which he could work by candlelight. Crouched next to him, Raven had hugged herself with her thin arms and warned him in a quavering voice, "the darkness is coming; it's going to be so cold," and he'd had no clue what she was talking about.

The blackness fell over him like a heavy drop cloth. An icy blast hit him, as if he'd been placed in the open doorway of a walk-in freezer. Fingers tingling from the sudden lowering of temperature, he dropped the shotgun shell he'd been mining for gunpowder.

The rush of coldness subsided as suddenly as it had come. But the darkness remained, gathered like a robe around their circle of candle flame. Although the sun had finally set, the nightfall that had settled over the land was deeper than any Nick had ever seen. Whatever strange enchantments that existed in Westbrook had enhanced the depth of the night, too.

"We've gotta be really careful now," Raven said.

Nick didn't ask why. *He's here*, he thought with a shudder. *It's his time now.*

Night creatures were singing. Nick heard the hoot of an owl, and sensed a fluttering of leathery wings above them in the treetops.

"We have enough of these," Nick said. He had hand-crafted five firecrackers, each one trailed by a narrow fuse. "Here, you take two of them, and some matches."

Raven stuffed the homemade explosives into her small, battered purse. They had taken several books of matches from the storehouse, and she kept one of those, too. As she filled her bag, she surveyed the night with a hooded gaze.

"We've got to get back to Westbrook," Nick said. "Is there a safe route back? Does he stick to the roads?"

"Nowhere is safe," she said. "But we stay away from the roads, for sure. He'll be out on his horse."

Nick remembered the horse, from his dream in the barn. How much of that feverish dream, as fantastical as it had been, might actually be real?

"And forget about this." Raven blew out their candle; darkness encroached in their space. "We've got to find our way without it."

"I can barely see my hand in front of my face," Nick said.

"I know the general direction." Raven grasped his hand. Her fingers were clammy with cool perspiration. "Once we start getting closer . . . you'll see what I mean."

They left behind their temporary refuge. Nick had put his own flash-bangs in his pockets along with matches; he carried the shotgun over his shoulder. He had only three shotgun shells remaining since he'd used the gunpowder in a few of them as fuel for his explosives. Every shot he had left needed to count.

Raven had Grandpa Lee's rifle, but only a handful of ammo, too.

Nick thought about his grandfather as they crept together through the woods. Had Grandpa Lee continued his strange nightly ritual of hunkering down in his house at nightfall, locking every window and door and waiting with a gun in his hands? His practice had seemed so nuts before, the eccentricity of an isolated old man—but Nick knew better, now. If he'd been forced to live on this land, with all its dark, terrible secrets, he would have done the same thing.

It ends tonight, Nick thought.

Raven stopped, and he nearly ran into her. His eyes had adjusted to the gloom; he saw her put her finger to her lips.

And then, she pointed.

He turned in the direction she indicated. At first, he didn't see anything: only trees wrapped in darkness. As he continued to stare, however, he made out a soft, orange glow, like the faint shimmer of a cigarette, floating slowly along on waves of blackness.

"His marker," Raven said in a tight whisper. Her mouth was right next to Nick's ear. "Always glowing. Remember that."

Nick swallowed. Although the glow came from perhaps a hundred yards away, he was afraid to speak for fear of being over-heard. His heart boomed at a rapid clip, and he had the crazy notion that the Overseer might hear that, too.

"Looking for us, you think?" Nick dared to ask. His voice was so low he barely heard his own words.

"He's looking for anyone who isn't marked," Raven said. "That's all he does, all night long 'til dawn. He searches. I try to stay far, far away from that glow. So should you."

He was about to tell her, *I can't; I have to kill him*, but kept quiet. He would have sounded like a frightened child claiming he was going to rip open the closet door and kill the bogeyman. A raw, superstitious fear had taken hold of him, and he wasn't sure how he would overcome it and perform the task that he knew in his heart waited in store for him.

They watched, still and silent, until the light drifted out of sight.

43

The magical restoration of the estate and its residents continued to dazzle Amiya. As Miss Lula led her back downstairs, Amiya took in the sights and sounds of the transformed world.

Every floorboard, every piece of wooden wall paneling, every chandelier, every curtain . . . all had been restored to glittering, lavish perfection. The air smelled not of ash and cinder, but of fine scents: richly carved wood, sumptuous food, sweet summer roses.

Amiya noticed details that had not been present on her earlier tour through the home—items that must have been destroyed by the fire. Vases, for one. There were so many crystal vases, of all colors and sizes, arrayed on tables and standing throughout candlelit rooms, and each of them housed the freshly cut roses that scented the air.

"Like what you see, lady?" Miss Lula asked. She wore a self-satis-fied smile, as if she herself were responsible for the splendor surrounding them. "Who would ever want to leave such a wonderful place?"

They passed the parlor, from which the piano chords floated. A young man attired in a tuxedo sat at the keyboard of the grand piano. Amiya did a double take: it was Ossie.

Ossie inclined his head toward Amiya, a slight acknowledgment of their burgeoning friendship.

"I thought he worked in the kitchen?" Amiya asked Miss Lula.

"He works wherever I want him to work," Miss Lula said. "I told him to play tonight, in honor of our new lady."

Amiya didn't know whether to laugh or scream at the absurdity of it all. It was as if she had tumbled into some nightmarish rendition of *Cinderella.*

Miss Lula brought her to the closed double doors of the dining room. She pushed open one of the doors with a flourish.

"The master is eager to meet you." Miss Lula took Amiya's hand in a firm grip, clearly sensing Amiya's apprehension. "Come inside."

She brought Amiya across the threshold. Amiya scanned the candlelit room, muscles coiled with tension—and then she saw him.

He stood at the big picture window on the far side of the chamber, his back facing her. Tall and broad-shouldered, he wore a black tailed tuxedo. Crisp white hair flowed to his shoulders in a smooth mane.

Amiya was certain she had never seen this man before. Had he come back with the house, too, rising from the grounds like some haunting spirit made into flesh?

"Master Westbrook," Miss Lula said. "Your lady has arrived."

Westbrook turned. He had that classic blue blood look about him: the soft features of a southern aristocrat who had never spent a day of his life engaged in anything more laborious than signing contracts. Amiya might have considered him handsome for an older gentleman, under any other circumstances.

But there was something not quite right about his appearance, and it took a moment for her to discern the key detail that hinted at his unearthly rebirth.

"My, my, my," Westbrook said, in a syrupy Georgia drawl. "You've outdone yourself this time, Miss Lula, yes, indeed."

He smiled, and Amiya's heart clutched.

His teeth—oh God, his teeth.

Westbrook's teeth were perfectly white—and honed to razor-sharp points.

Like a shark, she thought, a chill coursing through her that the warm room couldn't dispel.

Westbrook strode toward her, taking easy, smooth strides: the walk of a man confident in his domain. His blue-eyed gaze never left her face. But there was a *flatness* to his eyes, as if they had been painted on; the eyes of a wax figure, perhaps, that might appear genuine in a strictly physical sense, but lacked the depth of a living soul.

Every nerve ending in Amiya's body screamed at her to run out of the room, to escape the evil that this man wore about him as plainly as his tailored tuxedo. But she kept her high-heeled feet rooted to the floor.

It was time to play the game.

She noticed the bulge of a pistol riding his waist, and heard the soft jingle of keys with each of his footsteps.

"A fine lady, indeed." Lips peeled back in a broad smile, showing his sharklike teeth in full, Westbrook stepped to Amiya and took her hand.

Amiya suppressed a shiver. His skin was cold.

He bent and kissed her fingers. She felt the tip of his clammy tongue on her flesh, the hardness of his needlelike teeth. Nausea snaked through her.

"I'll leave you two to get acquainted," Miss Lula said. "Master Westbrook, we'll be serving dinner soon. Your favorite, of course."

"Thank you, Miss Lula," he said. He winked at his departing house manager. "This one's a keeper for sure."

"If she knows what's best for her." Miss Lula shot Amiya a warning glare. "Behave, lady."

"I'm fine." Amiya tried to smile, but she felt sick.

"I'll fetch you a drink, my lady," Westbrook said. "You look as if you could use one. Does bourbon suit you?"

Amiya rarely drank hard liquor, but she sensed that refusing the offer would be a mistake. "Yes, please. That sounds good."

Westbrook spun on his heel and ambled to the large oak liquor cabinet. Using a crystal decanter, he poured a finger of liquor each in two glasses.

"I trust my staff has treated you well during your stay." He returned to her and offered her the drink.

"They've been . . . fine," Amiya said, picking her words carefully. This man, or whatever he was, was the last one here that she could trust. "Quite accommodating."

"That's what I like to hear." He settled onto a nearby chaise lounge made of a smooth velour material. He patted a space next to him. "Sit, please." He flashed his predator's grin. "I don't bite."

Despite his assurances, looking at his mouthful of sharp teeth, it was much too easy for her to imagine him literally tearing her flesh apart, tendon by tendon, and consuming her raw. She had to forcibly eject the gruesome image from her mind.

Trying not to spill the drink because her hand was trembling, Amiya eased onto the furniture. She crossed her legs and balanced the glass on her knee, bracing it in both hands.

"Not much of a drinker, are you?" he asked. He chuckled, took a small sip from his glass. "Have a sip, sugar. It's excellent bourbon, distilled by a former business associate of mine."

She levered the rim of the glass against her lip, tilted it slightly, allowing the barest amount of liquor to touch her tongue. It was good whiskey as he promised, but she needed to keep a clear head.

"Nice," she said.

Westbrook nodded with approval. He unfolded his body across the chaise lounge, one of his legs only inches from hers.

"I keep a wine cellar as well," he said. "A large quantity of Bordeaux, top of the line quality. You look like the kind of lady who might appreciate that sort of thing."

"I enjoy red wine," she said, an honest answer.

"We'll open a bottle for dinner, then," Westbrook said. "I like a lady who appreciates the finer things in life that I can offer."

Amiya offered merely a brief smile and a nod. In her adult life, she had been on dates with dozens of men, and Westbrook reminded her of an older, wealthy gentleman that she'd once agreed to have dinner with when she was in her early twenties. Like Westbrook, he continually reminded her of his material possessions, the fine things he could bestow upon her, as if such things were all she cared about. She had smiled and nodded her way through the evening but generally kept him at arm's length, concluding the encounter by allowing him only a chaste kiss on her cheek.

She doubted the same strategy would work with Westbrook. He kept stretching and expanding his body, inching into her personal space. He knew she couldn't run away. She was in his world, and the penalties for rejecting his advances were severe.

As he was chatting about his wine cellar, he casually let his hand drop onto her thigh.

Amiya stifled a scream—but she couldn't resist stirring. His cold touch sent a current of ice through her bloodstream.

"Touchy, are you?" He grinned, but withdrew his hand into his lap. "I must apologize, lady. You're so beautiful you've made me forget my manners."

"It's okay," she said. "This is all so overwhelming."

"I understand," he said, though his flat eyes showed no awareness of her emotions. "You're here in this magical place, and you're wondering how is it all happening? Did you slip into a dream?"

Amiya said nothing, let him continue.

"I fade into sleep at dawn every morning and I don't remember a thing about it when I wake at sunset," Westbrook said. "Terrible things happened here, on my property, as you may have surmised, but the evidence of such things is washed away nightly. It's the blessing that we receive."

"The blessing?" she asked, and couldn't hide her sarcasm.

"*The blessing*," he repeated, and took a sip of whiskey. "You could have a highly regarded position in this house of mine. You could retire to your room and sleep away the day, and awaken to a dream each night. A dream of rich, sumptuous things and handsome gentlemen eager to please you." Chuckling, he made a sweeping gesture. "I have such pleasures to show you, my lady."

As if on cue, someone knocked on the doors across the room that led to the kitchen, and the doors swung inward on oiled hinges. A dapper young man entered. He pushed a small cart laden with silver and covered dishes.

Westbrook flashed a hungry smile and rose to his feet.

"Dinner is served," he said.

44

Nick spotted the Westbrook estate from hundreds of yards away, the lighted mansion floating like an electric cruise ship on a black sea. At the sight of it, he sucked in an involuntary gasp, as if he'd been kicked in the ribs.

"Yeah, that's what I was telling you about," Raven said, beside him. "Here, everything changes at night."

"Like how it was before the fire," he said. "According to my grandfather."

He saw her shadowed shape offer an indifferent shrug.

"I'm used to it," she said. "When I was living in that house, it became a regular thing. It's easy to forget how something makes no sense when it's your everyday reality."

"People can adapt to anything," Nick said. "Including what should be impossible."

"Yeah." Her face was a dark oval. "Now that we've got your fire-crackers, what do you want to do?"

"Let's get closer to the house and we'll figure out something," he said.

They advanced through the woods, the lights of the estate serving as a beacon in the darkness. Nick was equally aware of the need to look out for another light: the soft orange glow marking the Overseer's branding iron. He didn't see any evidence of the man, and assumed that he had drifted away to search another region of the property.

Soon, he would have to stop hiding from the Overseer and seek him out. The thought of that imminent confrontation literally gave him a physical sense of dread; a tight coiling of his abdomen muscles that made breathing difficult.

It's going to be the only way out, Nick thought. *When the time comes, I'll have to push through everything I'm feeling and look that man in the face.*

As the surrounding tree cover thinned, Nick slowed. Wrought-iron lanterns, equipped with flickering candles, had been posted at various spots along the path leading to the mansion. Those lights stood at numerous locations throughout the property, too.

Nick saw at least two people wandering the yard, crossing between patches of candlelight and shadow. They had the look of guards. Given all the trouble that Nick and Raven had given them today, they would be on high alert.

"We can try going around the back," Raven said. "There's a few small buildings close to the house, around a courtyard."

"Okay, I remember we saw those earlier."

Keeping to the trees, Raven made a beeline to their left, circling around the perimeter of the plantation complex. Although they were couched in darkness, they were close enough to the residence for Nick to pick up some of the noises issuing from within that carried on the cool night air: laughter, the clatter of dishes, soft piano notes.

"It sounds like they're having a party," Nick said.

"They are." Raven crept through weeds without turning. "Everyone looks forward to the night. I used to, like the rest of the house staff."

"What about the field hands?" Nick asked.

"They have time off in their quarters. They have parties, too. Some of them brew their own stuff to drink, I guess."

"Moonshine," Nick said.

"Yeah, that's what they call it. It was gross but they liked to drink it."

"With people outside partying in their slave quarters, someone had to get pregnant," Nick said. "Are there any babies here?"

"The Overseer takes them," Raven said, matter-of-factly. "I never saw it but I heard about it. A field hand had a baby at night and the Overseer went right into the cabin and took it as soon as it was born."

Nick's mind reeled. "He took the baby? What did he do with it?"

"I don't know, but we never saw it again," she said. She threw a look back at him, her eyes gleaming. "People try not to have babies. I heard Miss Lula will use a coat hanger if any woman in the house gets pregnant."

Nick felt ill, the watery weakness spreading to his knees. He had to rest against a tree for a moment, slowing drawing deep breaths.

"You okay?" Raven asked.

He wanted to scream at her. *Am I okay? You've shared with me that on my family's land, babies are stolen from mothers and the house manager is performing abortions with coat hangers? Sure, it's all good, girl. No worries.*

But he didn't yell at her. Raven had been steeped in Westbrook's bizarre subculture for many years, and had been desensitized to the horror that would have outraged anyone outside of the property's barbed wire fence.

He desperately needed to get her out of this place. He needed to get all of them out of this place.

Once he did, he might burn it all to the ground, destroying it by fire once more, and forever.

45

Dinner with Master Westbrook was a gut-wrenching affair for Amiya, and the loathsome experience began with the food. Not her food—the server brought her a platter of roast chicken, petite potatoes, and carrots—*his* food.

The dish set in front of him was some sort of thick stew in a deep porcelain bowl, and the broth was blood-red. She saw the raw head of a small, skinned animal still bearing its eyes—a squirrel, maybe—floating in its depths.

"Ah, Brunswick stew, my favorite." Westbrook snapped out a white cloth napkin and tucked it into his collar. He seemed oblivious to Amiya's disgust.

If she could have gotten up and fled out of the dining room she would have done so. But Westbrook had seated himself at the head of the long table and insisted on her sitting next to him. This would be yet another grin-and-bear-it tribulation she had to endure.

"Let us say grace," Westbrook said. He reached across the table for her hand.

She suppressed a wince at the coldness of his grip, bowed her head. Westbrook cleared his throat.

"Our ancient lords of darkness, we thank you for another night of celebration," Westbrook said. "We are grateful for the abundance you've granted us. I am grateful for yet another opportunity to open my eyes and appreciate the beauties of this world." He squeezed her hand at that, sending fresh spicules of ice through her blood. "May we bring honor to you on this fine night. Amen."

"Amen," Amiya said. She had mentally phrased her own, abbreviated prayer: *God, please give me the strength to keep on.*

"Now let's dig in. I feel as if I could eat a whole hog," Westbrook said, and dipped a big spoon into his bowl.

Amiya averted her gaze and focused on her own plate. She picked at the food, though she knew she probably should have tried to eat something; she had no idea when she might eat again if she tried to escape.

Another well-dressed server, a woman, brought a bottle of Bordeaux. Westbrook poured a glass for Amiya and insisted on her sampling it. The wine was superb, but Amiya had decided she couldn't allow herself to enjoy it, as she suspected that part of Westbrook's strategy to seduce her was straight out of the good ole boy handbook: get her drunk and turn her as pliable as putty in his cold, eager hands.

Westbrook's sharp teeth made quick work of the raw animal floating in his monstrous stew. Amiya heard him snapping bones in his mouth. The noises turned her stomach and she put down her fork for good.

Westbrook didn't appear to notice or care. He picked up his bowl with both hands and lifted it to his lips, slurping every last bloody drop, his Adam's apple bobbing with each disgusting swallow.

I could slit his throat, right now, Amiya thought. She envisioned the fine dark line she could slash across his neck with the blade, a clean cut of his carotid artery. She imagined the jet of hot, spurting blood . . .

But she hesitated, and the moment was lost.

Would slitting his carotid artery have had any effect, anyway? Did real blood stream through his veins? Did he possess a living, pulsing heart?

Westbrook placed the bowl back onto the table and dabbed at the corners of his lips with the napkin. He regarded her coolly, as if he'd been aware of her murderous thoughts all along.

"You're a tough nut to crack, my lady," he said.

She straightened in the chair. "Excuse me?"

"I don't think I've made much headway with you this evening. If things keep moving along like this, I don't think I'll get anywhere with you tonight, or anytime soon."

"Don't men of power appreciate a challenge?" She offered what she hoped was an inviting smile.

He chuckled. "You're a clever one. I might yet spare you the Overseer's mark for a while."

"Where is the Overseer?" She tried to mask her anxiety.

"He's not on the premises at this time, a fact for which all of you should be grateful," Westbrook said, in a lowered tone. He glanced over his shoulder at the windows.

"All of us?" Amiya asked. "But you're the master of the plantation. It bears your name."

"I couldn't expect you to understand these arcane matters," Westbrook said. He tossed back the remaining wine in his glass, picked up the bottle, and poured more for himself, and her, though her glass was still half-full.

"Try me," Amiya said. "I'm a quick learner."

"Indeed you are." Westbrook swirled the Bordeaux in his glass, deeply inhaled its bouquet. "The Overseer brokered the contract that makes all of this magic possible." He indicated the room with a sweeping gesture. "I am merely a beneficiary of the deal. I get to rise each sunset and wander the plantation, waxing nostalgic about the days of yore, and the staff refers to me as 'master' and pays me respect, and yes, I can romance beautiful maidens such as you. But this isn't my Westbrook anymore."

"It belongs to the Overseer," Amiya said.

"You are a bright one." Westbrook sipped his wine. His gaze never left her; those flat eyes drank in her body as deeply as he'd consumed the bowl of stew.

"Would you take me on a tour of the estate?" Amiya asked.

"A tour?" Westbrook's lips folded into a frown. "I was intending to take you to my private quarters."

"There's plenty of time for that, I'd say." She batted her eyelashes, and she saw his face brighten with interest. "I've been sequestered in a bedroom for most of the day. I'd love for you to show me around and tell me about your days of yore."

"The lady asks, and she shall receive." Westbrook tossed his napkin onto the table and rose from his chair, wineglass in hand. He offered his free arm to her and flashed his shark's grin. "I'm happy to oblige."

46

Remaining in the sheltering cover of the woods, Nick and Raven had circled to the back of the estate.

The rear was as well illuminated as the front, with lanterns spaced at regular intervals. The candlelight revealed a series of smaller interconnected structures that flanked the mansion: a kitchen, laundry, smokehouse, and other facilities. They flanked a grassy courtyard dominated by an elaborately designed wooden gazebo.

"It's actually beautiful," Nick whispered to Raven.

"At night," Raven said.

Nick didn't see any of the so-called helpers posted outdoors. He looked toward the house. Several large plate glass windows fronted the back wall of the residence. From his vantage point, Nick could see what was going on inside: well-dressed house staff bustling back and forth from one room to the next.

"There's a lot going on in there," Nick said. "Is that normal?"

Raven was about to answer when she pointed and let out a soft gasp. Nick felt as if his legs had been swept from underneath him.

He saw Amiya.

His girlfriend strolled along a corridor or room that placed her at the back windows of the house. She looked stunning in a red dress, and carried a glass of wine in a casual manner that he remembered from so many nights they had spent together.

She walked arm-in-arm with a tall, white-haired man who wore a black tuxedo. The man was chatting, gesturing expansively. Amiya was hanging on every word, like an ingénue dazzled by a worldly gentleman.

"I don't believe it," Nick said.

"She's the master's new lady," Raven said. "I thought that would happen when I heard about them taking her to the house."

"That's Westbrook?" Nick asked. He stared at the walking, talking White man, who should have been a heap of ash in a grave, and on some subconscious level he still found it difficult to accept that such a thing was possible.

"He comes out at night, like the Overseer," Raven said. "He does it for the women—that's all he cares about."

Nick saw Amiya laugh at something Westbrook said. He felt sick to his stomach.

Come on, babe, look out here and see me, Nick thought, wishing he could have telepathically sent those words to Amiya. He needed her to realize that he was alive and plotting to free her, to free all of them.

But Amiya didn't glance toward the windows, and if she had, he doubted she would have spotted him, concealed in foliage.

Westbrook had lowered one hand to the small of Amiya's back as he guided her along. Such an intense wave of anger tore through Nick that it took all of his self-control for him to stay still.

"The master is a phony," Raven said. "He acts like he's some nice guy, but she shouldn't trust him. He's going to take her to his bedroom and hurt her."

"She's got to be playing him, then," Nick said, more to himself than to Raven. "She knows how to read people, better than I do. She's got to be manipulating him."

"Probably," Raven said. A note of doubt colored her tone. "She sure looks like she's having fun."

Chattering like a couple on a first date, Amiya and Westbrook passed from view. Nick felt his stomach twist.

"We've got to get her out of there," he said.

He fished in his pockets and brought out the matches, and a flash-bang.

47

I'm having such a great time with this man, Amiya thought.

That was the idea that Amiya kept balanced at the uppermost surface of her mind. She hoped it translated to the expression on her face, the shine in her eyes, the ripple in her laughter, the roll of her hips. She needed Westbrook to believe he was winning her over, that his conquest was advancing successfully toward a long night of sexual decadence in his private quarters.

Secretly, she intended to kill him before such a thing could happen. Her success in that endeavor would hinge on timing and opportunity.

He led her on a tour through the estate, and she oohed and ahhed at all of the appropriate moments, and she took small sips of her wine. In between such things, she studied the musculature of Westbrook's pale neck and contemplated the knife resting deep in her pocket.

She could have slit his throat in the dining room, but it would have been the wrong place. She needed somewhere more private.

What surprised her was that she felt no compunctions about the idea of killing him. She realized that his very existence was an affront against nature; he had no business walking the earth and was long overdue for a permanent grave. That made the prospect of murdering him infinitely easier, from a moral perspective.

She kept those ideas mostly suppressed as he showed off his possessions, and Westbrook seemed fooled by her act. Like many men with narcissistic tendencies, he believed he was irresistible to women anyway. Her growing acquiescence to his supposed charms meant she was merely falling in line as he expected she would.

After he had shown off his art collection in the parlor, she smiled, and in a voice she hoped made her sound slightly tipsy (and perhaps she was), she said: "How about taking me to the wine cellar and showing me your fabulous collection of Bordeaux?"

"A lady after my own heart," Westbrook said and paid her a crooked grin.

He led her to another wing of the mansion. As they traveled along the gleaming hardwood corridors, he let his hand trail to the small of her back. When she offered no resistance by swaying out of his reach, he got bolder: he smoothed his palm across her undulating hips, teeth exposed in his shark's grin.

Just you wait, Amiya thought. *I've got something for you, mister eager hands.*

Westbrook brought her to a carved oak door at the end of the long corridor. A brass handheld lantern stood on a small table near the door, the flame already flickering. Westbrook removed a silver loop of keys from his pocket.

"The good stuff is kept under lock and key, hmm?" Amiya asked. She paid close attention to the key he used to disengage the padlock on the hasp.

"The best of my collection, yes." Westbrook unlocked the door and drew it open. Blackness yawned beyond the doorway. The cool air carried the rich scents of oak and raw earth.

Westbrook picked up the lantern, clasping his wineglass in his other hand.

"Stay close behind me, lady," he said. "You could trip on the steps down here without a light."

They started through the doorway, but were stopped by a voice.

"Master Westbrook?" Miss Lula said.

The house manager hurried toward them along the hallway, long arms swinging, pearls bouncing on her heavy bosom.

Shit, Amiya thought, and tried to conceal her frustration. *What does she want now?*

"Yes?" Westbrook paused on the threshold, eyebrows raised. "I'm a bit preoccupied at the moment, Miss Lula."

"Sir, I saw you coming this way. Is there something you need the staff to retrieve from the wine cellar?"

"I'm taking the lady on a tour," Westbrook said. He winked at Amiya. "She requested to see my Bordeaux."

"Did she now?" Miss Lula's gaze slid over to Amiya. A scowl settled over her features. There was no mistaking it: she suspected Amiya was up to no good.

Amiya offered up her best innocent smile. Miss Lula's scowl deepened.

"The lady has an appreciation for the finer things," Westbrook said. "What is your concern, Miss Lula?"

Miss Lula blinked. "If it pleases you, sir, I'll wait here at the open doorway. In case you need anything."

"I've already got everything I need for the evening." Westbrook scanned Amiya from head to toe, openly undressing her with his gaze. "But suit yourself, my dear."

Westbrook turned away. Amiya started to turn but Miss Lula tapped her shoulder.

"Behave, lady," Miss Lula said with a narrowed gaze. "I'll be up here listening, and I have a very keen sense of hearing."

Amiya responded with an indifferent shrug, but the woman's suspicion was going to complicate matters. She followed Westbrook onto the wide, descending staircase. Her heels clicked on the stone steps. The lantern flame cast huge, shifting shadows on the rock walls.

"This is my favorite area of the house," Westbrook said. He paused, glanced over his shoulder at her, blue eyes twinkling in the candlelight. "Well, after the bedroom."

He's laying it on thick now, Amiya thought. *This guy really believes he's going to get lucky tonight.*

They reached the bottom of the staircase. The temperature had dropped at least ten degrees. The cellar was a wide, low-ceilinged space with a smooth stone floor. A wooden barrel stood just ahead, in the center of the room. On three sides—back, right, and left— wooden wine racks were built into the walls. A bottle occupied nearly every slot, hundreds of them. They glimmered darkly in the flickering light.

"This is impressive," Amiya said.

"Isn't it?" Westbrook strolled to the barrel and placed his lantern on top of it. He gestured toward the bottles. "Have a gander, lady. If you find one that intrigues you, we'll select it for our next round."

Down here, the walls muted the din of the household. Amiya assumed the obverse of that perception held true: anything that took place in the cellar would go unheard by anyone on the upper levels of the residence.

But how much would Miss Lula detect while posted at the open doorway?

Her heart thudding a slow *lub-dub,* Amiya stepped to a wall of bottles. She was no expert in Bordeaux; one bottle was as good as another in her limited experience, and presumably Westbrook had acquired only vintages worth owning. She ran her fingers along the necks of the bottles, pulled out one after another to glance at the labels. All of them, of course, were written in French, a language for which she possessed only a middling fluency.

She finally picked one that she thought she could understand. She slid the bottle out of the slot and presented it to Westbrook.

"This one," she said. "Château Marguax."

"A fine selection." Westbrook nodded his approval. "While we're down here, I think I'll go ahead and pick another that I was thinking about as I was standing here."

Westbrook brushed past her, his hair rustling like dry leaves. His back to her, he contemplated the collection of bottles.

Amiya had slid her hand into her pocket and clasped the knife handle. Her fingers trembled. She gauged the distance between her body and his, the length of her arm, the height of his neck.

"Aha," Westbrook said. "Château Lafite. You'll love this one, too, my lady."

He drew the bottle out of the rack and turned around, a grin plastered on his pale face.

Using a backhand motion, a movement she had mastered from years of playing competitive tennis, Amiya whisked the edge of the blade across his neck. The cutting made a sound like scissors tearing through paper.

Westbrook's lips froze in the midst of his shark smile.

"I thought . . . we were getting along well, lady," he said softly.

He collapsed to the stone floor, blood pumping out of his carotid artery in great dark gouts. As he fell, the bottle flipped out of his hands and bounced against the stone with a clang, but the glass did not break. The wine rolled against the floor and came to rest at the edge of the barrel.

Amiya exhaled. Her heart slammed painfully.

"Is everything okay down there?" Miss Lula asked.

Hurrying, Amiya bent and searched Westbrook's still body. She located the set of keys. More important to her immediate needs, she found the gun, too.

"Master Westbrook?" Miss Lula called out.

Westbrook's gun was a silver revolver with a pearl handle. It looked like an antique, but she quickly figured out how to swing open the cylinder. The gun was already loaded.

Miss Lula was descending the staircase, heavy footsteps clopping against stone.

Amiya snapped the cylinder back into place. Holding the revolver in both hands, finger curled around the trigger, she rose just as Miss Lula reached the bottom of the staircase.

"You—" Miss Lula started to say, mouth spreading into a large "o" of shock.

The booming gun cut off her sentence as Amiya shot her point blank in the chest. The gun's report was painfully loud in the cellar, punishing Amiya's eardrums.

Letting out a sharp cry, Miss Lula rocked backward against the wall, bottles of wine clinking in her wake.

But she did not go down. Her eyes glowed with fire.

"Gonna have to do better than that, lady," she said.

With a grunt, she began to push herself upright.

Amiya dashed across the cellar, high heels clacking. The shoes slowed her down, and she kicked them off.

Snarling like a bear, Miss Lula lunged for her. With her long arm, she was able to snag the hem of Amiya's dress. She yanked. Fabric ripped, and Amiya spun around like a top, losing her balance. She tumbled to the floor. The gun clattered out of her grasp and slid away into the shadows.

"I knew you couldn't be trusted, bitch." Miss Lula lurched toward her, blood soaking the front of her dress.

Amiya scrambled across the floor. The nearest item in her vicinity was the bottle of Bordeaux that had fallen against the barrel. Screaming, she grabbed the neck of it and swung around with all the strength she could summon into her arm.

The meat of the bottle smashed against Miss Lula's head. Glass shattered, and fragrant red wine flew in a dark spray. Eyes rolling up to expose the whites, Miss Lula dropped to her knees with a soft moan.

Down, but not dead, Amiya thought.

Amiya raced past her, the torn dress rippling like flames around her legs. She reached the bottom of the staircase and hustled up the steps, the stone cold against her bare feet, but she had so much adrenaline surging through her bloodstream she barely felt it.

She burst through the doorway. She looked around for the padlock but couldn't see it, realized Miss Lula had probably taken it with her to keep herself from getting locked in, ever the calculating house manager.

Downstairs in the darkness, Miss Lula bellowed, sounding like some creature from an abyss. Soon, she would be back.

Amiya turned and saw Ossie rushing toward her down the long corridor. Perspiration glistened on his face. His eyes were wild with excitement.

"Someone's setting off bombs!" he shouted. "Everyone's running around like crazy!"

Nick, Amiya thought immediately, and felt such an intense crush of emotion that if Nick had been nearby, she would have smothered him in kisses.

She grabbed the sleeve of Ossie's tuxedo jacket.

"Come on, that's our signal to get out of here," she said.

48

fter igniting a flash-bang in the gazebo at the back of the house, Nick and Raven slipped inside the estate through the doors to the laundry. The eruption was louder than he'd expected, like a series of cherry bombs detonating, but he didn't want to wait around to assess the response to the explosions. They needed to take immediate advantage of whatever confusion the fireworks created.

The laundry was one of the support structures that flanked the courtyard. Raven assured him that in the evenings it was usually empty of staff.

Inside that dank chamber, a brass wall sconce equipped with a wavering candle provided the only light. Nick saw big steel wash basins on the floor, and piles of linens sitting on a long table. Old-fashioned washboards leaned against a wall, soap congealing on their ridges. There wasn't a washing machine or clothes dryer in sight.

This place is literally frozen in time, Nick thought.

"I lasted a day working in here before Miss Lula moved me." Raven sneered. "Hard, nasty work."

They threaded past the wash basins and table and reached a pair of double doors on the far side of the room. Nick heard commotion outside the room: muffled shouts and the patter of rapid footsteps.

"They're freaking out in there," he said.

Raven pushed open the doors. They swung out soundlessly.

The doors led to a wide but short hardwood corridor lit by a couple more wall sconces with candles. Another hallway intersected the passage.

A woman in a dress ran past shrieking, her hair wild and eyes swimming with terror. She didn't notice them standing there with their guns. She rushed past without slowing.

"What's the matter with them?" Nick asked.

"Some of these people have been here a really long time." Raven hurried forward clutching the rifle. "I guess your fireworks sort of woke them up."

At the intersection, she cut to the left. It would take them in the direction they had seen Amiya headed with Westbrook. Raven guessed that Westbrook had taken Amiya to the wine cellar, which everyone knew was one of his favorite areas of the mansion.

Nick had been amazed at the exterior condition of the restored estate, but inside, traveling down these polished hardwood corridors, seeing the crystal chandeliers ablaze with candlelight, and passing through the sumptuously furnished rooms . . . it called into question all his years of scientific study. If they survived this night, he would be forced to seriously reevaluate some beliefs that he had once held so dear and sacred.

The residents behaved as if they were out of their minds. He saw men and women, all of them dressed as if attending a black-tie affair. Babbling and shouting and weeping, they stampeded aimlessly through the house, and those that noticed Nick and Raven shrank away from them fearfully.

"We're here to help them, but they're looking at us as if they're scared," Nick said.

"Some of them we won't be able to help." Raven strode forward. "Like I said, they've been here too long."

"Institutionalized." He swept his gaze around. "I want to offer them a way out, but I need to find Amiya first."

"Right around the corner." Raven nodded toward an intersecting corridor ahead.

A man and a woman flashed through the intersection of hallways that Raven had indicated. Nick did a double take.

"Babe?" he asked.

Amiya turned, and saw him.

"Oh, God . . . Nick."

They ran into each other's arms.

49

Nick could have held Amiya in his arms for an eternity. She felt so vital, so alive—as if she were the only thing in his life that was truly real. He buried his face in her hair, and she twined her arms around his back. Her body shook with sobs, and he realized that he was crying, too.

There were others standing around them, but at that moment, none of that mattered to Nick. One of his unspoken fears had been that he would never hold Amiya in his arms again. It took feeling her body against him to draw the true depths of his emotions to the surface. They had stunned him to silence.

"I love you," Amiya whispered. "You have no idea how much."

"I'm so sorry," he said, his breaths getting snagged in his chest. Tears blinded him. "I'm so sorry, baby."

"Nothing to be sorry for," she said.

"I need to tell you why I wanted to sell the land. The truth."

Amiya drew back, blinking away tears. She put her finger against his lips.

"You wanted the money, for whatever reason you lied about," she said. "It doesn't matter anymore. What's going on here is so much bigger, Nick."

"I need to tell you."

"Then tell me when we're back home, safe." Worry tainted her eyes. "We're not out of the woods here yet."

"I promise I will, babe."

"Your granddad?" she asked, after a hesitation. "Did you ever find him?"

"He's back home. It's a long story. But he knows what's going on out here and I'm going to put an end to it for good."

From somewhere behind them, Nick heard a scream. It wasn't like the cries of hysteria issuing from the long-term captives of the estate. It was a shriek of unholy rage.

"That's Miss Lula," Raven said.

"She's pissed off for real," the young man who had been with Amiya said. He glanced at Nick. "I'm Ossie. You set off the bomb, didn't you?"

"Homemade fireworks," Nick said. "You know Raven?"

"I got stuck here after she got out, but I've heard about her." He gave Raven a brief smile. "You're kinda like a legend here."

"Good to know, but we better get out of here, y'all," Raven said. "When Miss Lula comes through that door down the hall, she's gonna be like a hurricane."

"Let her come, then." Nick pumped the shotgun. "I've done enough running."

50

The fearsome house manager known as Miss Lula emerged through the darkened doorway of the wine cellar. She was taller than Nick, and broad-shouldered, with long, heavy arms. Blood covered her face as if a bucket of it had been poured over her head, and a dark stain had spread across her wide bosom.

Despite her apparent injuries, she displayed no awareness of pain. Her eyes seethed with an unquenchable fury, a hunger to dispense severe suffering.

Miss Lula swept her gaze across all of them. Heart knocking, Nick stepped forward. She settled her attention on him.

"You're the field hand they caught today." Miss Lula glowered. "You got no business here in the master's house. You don't know your place, little man."

She gripped a straight razor. Lantern light glinted on the blade's deadly, honed edge.

"I don't want to shoot you," Nick said. "Stand down and let us leave in peace, ma'am. Please."

"You ain't going nowhere except back out in those fields, boy."

"Don't make me do this." Nick raised the shotgun to his shoulder.

Miss Lula merely smiled.

"You think I haven't been shot before, field hand?" She advanced toward him, arms swinging.

The woman's confidence unnerved Nick. In a place such as this, where so much defied the laws of science, could he really expect a load of buckshot to have the intended effect?

"Nick," Amiya said behind him, as if she had picked up on his fear.

Miss Lula lifted the razor above her head.

Nick squeezed the trigger.

The shotgun blazed and bucked. A spray of buckshot hit Miss Lula at center mass, knocked her back, and brought her to her knees.

Head lowered, she panted, trembled.

"Back off!" Nick pumped the shotgun.

Miss Lula raised her head. Her face was a vision of rage.

Hurt, but still mad as hell. Good God.

Grimacing, she came at him again.

Nick fired another shot. The buckshot spun her around as if she had been shoved by a gust of wind. She crashed against the wall, one arm striking an oil painting and sending it flying to the floor. She staggered, but gathered her bearings before she fell.

Nick trembled. He had only one shotgun shell left. He pumped the weapon.

Shrieking, Miss Lula raced toward him and drew back her arm to swing the razor.

Nick shot her in the head. The buckshot tore away the top of her skull. Bits of brain matter, hair, and blood spattered wetly against the walls and ceiling. Eyes wide as if with surprise, Miss Lula fell to the hardwood with a heavy thud. The straight razor tumbled out of her twitching fingers.

Breathless, Nick backed away. His ears rang. His hands felt numb on the shotgun. He let it sag out of his grip and clunk against the floor.

Around him, everyone in the house had fallen silent. He turned and saw awestruck expressions, as if he had just poured a pail of water over the wicked witch and shrunk her into nothingness.

"She's dead," Amiya finally said softly. She reached for Nick's hand. "Can we go now?"

51

There were other helpers serving the Overseer, but with Miss Lula's killing, none of them presented any resistance. After Amiya hurried to a bedroom upstairs and dressed in her own clothing, Nick, Amiya, Raven, and Ossie strode to the front doors of Westbrook and flung them open. No one said a thing or made a move to stop them.

"All of you can leave," Amiya said to the house staff. "No one's going to keep you imprisoned here anymore. Someone needs to tell the so-called field hands, too."

The captives milled around inside and didn't follow them to the doorway. To Nick, they looked lost and fearful. The psychological trauma they had endured might have damaged many of them beyond repair. Others would surely need extensive counseling to rejoin the ranks of citizens in the ordinary world.

"There's one more thing I have to do before they can leave," Nick said to Amiya. "I've got to deal with the Overseer."

"Why?" Fear pinched Amiya's features.

"We're marked," Raven said. "The Overseer's brand keeps us here. We'd all die if we tried to leave."

"That's what I've heard, too," Ossie said.

Amiya was shaking her head in either disagreement or disbelief.

"I've seen it, it's true," Nick said. "There's no other way. It's my responsibility, my family's obligation."

"I don't want to believe any of it," Amiya said. She pressed her lips together, closed her eyes for a beat, as if gathering her resolve. She looked at him. "But I'll follow you wherever you go, Nick."

The significance of her newfound faith in him wasn't lost on Nick. A month ago, he had proposed to her and she had declined. He hadn't earned her trust; he realized that now. He hadn't shown himself worthy of a lifetime commitment.

All of that had changed in less than a day, triggered by the most unlikely series of events imaginable. He was determined to validate her belief in him. He would show her he was the kind of man who would put it all on the line, not to fulfill his own selfish desires, but for the benefit of his family and all that was right in the world.

"I'm kind of surprised the Overseer isn't here already," Raven said. "With everything that's been going on. Something like this should've gotten his attention."

"I have to go to him," Nick said.

Raven blinked. "Go to his house? Umm, no way. You remember what happened last time, don't you?"

"It's exactly why I need to go there again." Nick took in the confused, frightened looks among the gathered group. "And I need to do it alone. This is a family matter."

"I don't understand," Amiya said.

"I don't know if I understand it all yet, either. But I know what I've got to do." He stepped forward and gave Amiya a light kiss on the lips. Then, he dug the remaining flash-bangs and matches out of his pockets and gave them to her as she stared at him with a confused frown.

"Hang onto these," he said. "I'll be back soon. Promise."

52

Wandering like a phantom through the night, Nick traveled to the Overseer's house. A widely spaced series of lanterns illuminated the narrow dirt path along the way.

He had no weapons. He'd left the shotgun back at the estate, having run out of ammo anyway, and he'd let the others keep the rifle. Neither of those firearms would have been any use in a fight against the Overseer.

He didn't know how he understood such things. A powerful sense of intuition guided him. It overrode reason, logic.

Maybe he was just too tired to think anymore. Emotionally, mentally, and physically, this had been the most grueling day of his entire life.

It's not over yet. The most difficult part is yet to come.

He came around a bend in the path. The Overseer's small house lay ahead, standing within a grove of trees. It had been restored just as the other structures had been. Flickering light shone through the front window.

His grandfather's pickup truck was parked near the house. The vehicle looked thoroughly anachronistic in such a setting; it was akin to discovering a rocket ship in the midst of a remote African village.

Nick slowed his pace, his feet suddenly feeling as if they were cast in lead. He didn't want to find out why Grandpa Lee had crossed over the bridge and come to the Overseer's house. Grandpa Lee was supposed to be home, locked in for the night. He didn't belong here.

All of us bear the curse . . .

Despite his dread, Nick's feet carried him forward. Crossing the yard, he walked past his grandfather's truck. A tarp covered the flatbed, something that hadn't been there earlier when they'd driven the pickup . . . but Nick averted his gaze from the vehicle, unwilling to consider what his granddad's presence here meant to him, meant to everything.

To set them free, you have to kill him . . .

The porch's floorboards were firm under his feet, though he felt as if he might collapse at any moment. He dropped his hand on the doorknob.

He turned it, pushed open the door.

The Overseer stood across the room, in front of a flickering hearth. He looked over his shoulder at Nick.

"Welcome home, son," his grandfather said.

53

Nick stepped inside the house slowly, as if caught in a fever dream. He carefully shut the door behind him.

He didn't trust himself to speak without screaming, so he said nothing.

The interior of the house had been reinvented, but it contained few furnishings. A dresser with a mirror, table, a bed that looked as if it had never been used. The only light in the room issued from the flames dancing in the fireplace; two chairs flanked the hearth.

Grandpa Lee wore the Overseer's complete set of clothes: the brown Stetson hat, black pea jacket, and dusty leather boots. The clothing fit as if it had been tailored to his measurements. Perhaps it had, yet another aspect of the malicious magic at work in this place.

"I knew you'd come soon," Grandpa Lee said. He turned back to the fire, knelt in front of it. He manipulated some sort of tool that he had placed in the flames. Nick shuffled forward, hesitant, and saw that it was exactly what he had feared.

The branding iron.

Nick finally spoke.

"It's been you, all this time?" he asked.

"It's been *us*," Grandpa Lee said. "Before me, my father. For me, it goes all the way back to Great-Great-Great Granddaddy John. John was the first who actually served at Westbrook—the Overseer. He took the devil's bargain and cursed us all."

Upon entering the room, Nick had felt dizzy. But the vertigo had faded, replaced by a sharp sense of horrifying clarity.

Hadn't he always known, in his heart, that his grandfather was at the root of what was going on? The bizarre behavior as nightfall approached, the staunch refusal to ever consider selling the property, or to even allow outsiders onto the land? All of it had been evidence of the deepest of secrets that Granddad had been keeping for so many years.

"You knew it, son," Grandpa Lee said. "It's written in your eyes."

"You come over here, every night," Nick said. "To put on these old clothes and terrify the prisoners you're keeping here."

"They deserve . . . *punishment*," Grandpa Lee said, his voice dropping several octaves. His eyes growing unfocused as if he had slipped into a trance, he moved his hand to the whip holstered like a handgun on the waist of his jacket. "Split open the skin on their backs and let the blood flow with their tears. Pain is the best teacher; it instills discipline."

"Grandpa Lee? That's not what you believe; that's not who you are."

Hearing his name uttered reeled him back. He blinked, shuddered, eased into a chair near the fire.

Nick sat in the wooden chair on the other side of the fireplace. Grandpa Lee gazed into the dancing flames. The business end of the branding iron, resting in the rippling lip of the fire, glowed orange.

"You've got to let them go," Nick said. "Set them free, and set yourself free, Grandpa. Leave this place for good."

"Sell it to the corporate masters and watch them tear down the trees and build monuments to the new gods of capitalism?" Grandpa Lee chuckled, and his gaze narrowed. "Have you learned nothing here today, son?"

"There are people here, suffering. You have the power to let them go."

"They've got the mark," Grandpa Lee said, nodding toward the simmering branding iron. "That tool, most of all . . . that's where the power resides. Enchanted by the ancient entities who feasted on our pain, channeling their magic."

"Don't ever touch it again, then," Nick said.

But as Grandpa Lee studied the iron, a tremor passed through him. His eyelids fluttered, and he spoke to Nick in a tense whisper. "You have no clue how it feels to press that iron to bare flesh. To see that symbol *cooked* into their skin for eternity. You smell the flesh burning, such a sweet aroma, the scent of undiluted power."

Fingers trembling, he bent forward to grasp the iron. Nick propelled himself off the chair and lunged at his grandfather.

Together, they fell to the hard floor. They rolled like drunken wrestlers, dangerously close to the flames. Nick pinned his granddad underneath him.

"Kill me, son," Grandpa Lee whispered. He did not attempt to fight back. Tears tracked down his face and drained to the floor in fat rivulets. "End this. Do it. Please."

"I can't," Nick said.

His face contorting into a rictus of rage, Grandpa Lee tried to push Nick off and reach for the iron. Nick batted his hand away.

"I won't let you," Nick said. "Not anymore."

And he grabbed the iron's wooden handle.

54

Amiya was worried.

She never should have consented to Nick wandering off, alone, to single-handedly confront the Overseer. She'd been overcome by a temporary stroke of madness to agree to such a thing. Nick had sounded confident, full of profound insights that he had gained over his time there, but he was nevertheless alone. After all the trials they had endured just to find each other again, it seemed ridiculous that she hadn't gone with him.

She had decided to go look for him. Their new friends, Raven and Ossie, came with her.

Walking shoulder to shoulder, they traveled on the dirt path that wound about the plantation property. Lanterns lit their way, the flames casting circles of orange-golden light. The air was cool and crisp against her skin.

It would have been a relaxing stroll through the night if not for the dread that lay like a stone against her heart.

The teenage girl, Raven, had offered to give the rifle back to Amiya. Amiya told her to keep it. Raven had smiled with gratitude.

Amiya didn't need another gun. She still had the revolver she had taken from Westbrook, but after her violent confrontations with him and Miss Lula, Amiya didn't want any more blood on her hands. If Nick knew what he was doing, none of them would have to fight again.

But instinct, which had kept her alive this long, warned her that more trouble lay ahead.

None of them spoke as they advanced along the road, their shoes kicking up little puffs of dust and stones. All of them were wired with tension, for their own reasons.

"What's the first thing you plan to do when you get out of here?" Amiya asked. She put the question to them to try to ease everyone's minds—including her own.

"I want a shower," Raven said. "And I want to put on some fresh clothes." She gestured at the dress she wore, which had been restored to a state of newness like everything else. "This feels like a prison uniform to me."

"I feel you," Ossie said. He pulled at the lapel of his tuxedo. "I can hardly wait to get out of this and put on some regular gear. But I want to see my family most of all."

"Your mother?" Amiya asked.

Ossie nodded, swallowed. "She was sick when I got here. Cancer. I hope she's still . . ."

"She'll be okay," Raven said. "God isn't that cruel."

"Yeah," Ossie said, bobbing his head in agreement. "I gotta believe that."

It amazed Amiya that despite the awful things these people had witnessed, they could still express hope. She hadn't had the opportunity to assemble her thoughts on how the things she had seen fit into her personal worldview. But the resiliency of these people, who had endured far more at Westbrook than she had, lifted her spirits.

She was about to share with them her first intent upon getting out of here, when a sudden noise derailed her thoughts.

"What's that sound?" she asked. "It sounds like a horse galloping, maybe?"

Raven stopped as if she had run into a wall. Terror flashed in her eyes.

"It's *him*," she said.

Ossie seized Amiya's arm and pulled her off the road. She was so surprised by the fear that had come over both of them that she didn't resist. All three of them scrambled into the forest that bordered the path, plunging into veils of concealing darkness.

From what they hoped was a safe distance, they crouched in the undergrowth, and watched the road.

"I don't understand," Amiya said in a whisper. "Nick said he was going to *stop* the Overseer."

"He couldn't do it," Ossie said. "Nobody can."

"Be quiet," Raven said in a tight voice. "He's close."

The sound of hooves striking dirt grew louder. Through the trees, Amiya saw the animal and its rider draw into view. The figure wore a wide-brimmed hat that kept his facial features hidden in shadow, but he carried something that glowed bright orange with latent heat.

Branding iron, Amiya realized, fear clamping over her gut like a vise.

The Overseer brought his horse to a halt in the section of the road that Amiya and her group had just vacated. His head swiveled back and forth slowly.

He knows we're here, Amiya thought.

Beside her, Raven whimpered.

In one smooth motion, the Overseer dismounted. In one hand, he carried the glowing iron. In the other, he unfurled what looked like a whip.

He strode to the edge of the forest.

Raven screamed, and fled. Ossie shot to his feet. He tugged Amiya's arm.

"We gotta go!" he said.

Amiya was terrified, but intuition had frozen her in place. There was something frighteningly familiar about the Overseer, how he carried himself. She knew this man, as unlikely as it seemed, and she knew him intimately.

Alerted by Raven's scream, the Overseer had spun in their direction. He snapped the whip, and it was as if he were a mythical god wielding a jagged bolt of blue lightning. Sizzling, the whip crackled against a tree. The tree snapped in half as if formed of balsa wood, and the woods suddenly seethed with acrid smoke.

"Come on!" Ossie shouted.

Amiya tore her gaze away from the Overseer and took off running.

55

The Overseer stalked his quarry through the woods. Two of them were runaways. The other was a woman, not yet marked, who needed to be added to his stable.

All of them deserved punishment. Pain was the most effective teacher, the surest way to instill discipline and everlasting fear.

He snapped the whip through the trees. Trunks split and toppled in his wake. He strode through the wreckage, wood chips flying and smoke curling and twisting about him.

He heard his quarry screaming, and their cries of terror invigorated him. He drank deeply of their fear.

Run, run, run. Run for your very lives. I will capture you and punish you for your disobedience, and in your nightmares you'll still be running from me.

They had a lead on him, but it mattered not at all. Westbrook and all of the land around it belonged to him, and it was night, his time.

There was nowhere to run.

Nowhere to hide.

56

They were running blindly through the woods. It was so dark Amiya could barely see her hands in front of her face. The only notable light came from behind them: the flashes of crackling blue lightning when the Overseer lashed his otherworldly whip. Each pulse of bluish light brightened the woods for a heartbeat, created leaping images that lingered in Amiya's vision like aftereffects of flashes from a camera.

She had been tanked on adrenaline, but fatigue had begun to take its toll on her. Her thigh muscles burned. Her lungs ached. She badly needed to take a breather, just for a few minutes.

But the Overseer kept coming, unrelenting. He was walking, not running. But for every stride she took more slowly, he seemed to take more quickly, as if he were siphoning her strength, fueled by her growing fear.

I know who he is but I can't believe it because it's impossible . . .

Raven and Ossie were faltering, too. Ossie had stumbled, and Amiya had needed to grab his arm and pull him up. Raven, fighting through the undergrowth, somehow had lost the rifle in a tangle of vines. They were in too much of a hurry to look for it, and like

Amiya, probably believed the gun wouldn't have helped them anyway.

"Keep going, guys," Amiya said. Her throat felt raw, like an open wound. She grabbed a fistful of Ossie's tuxedo jacket and tugged him onward. He groaned.

"Think I twisted my ankle," he said. Panting, he leaned against a tree, his body a slim silhouette. "Just . . . just keep going. Don't let me hold you up."

"I'm not leaving you behind," Amiya said. "Think about Tanya. Don't you want to see your mother again?"

"Huh?" He sucked in a pained breath.

"She means, move it!" Raven said. She had gone on ahead of them. In a flash of gas-jet blue light, her face was a mask of fear. "Man up!"

Cursing, Ossie pushed away from the tree. He snagged Amiya's arm, leaned his weight against her.

Amiya glanced over her shoulder. The Overseer continued to close the distance as he cut a wide swath through the woods. His branding iron glowed brighter than ever, as if in anticipation of searing her flesh.

She pulled Ossie along. He groaned, but followed. Her feet ached, her shins plagued by splinters of pain as she trod over the uneven terrain. It had been such a long, agonizing day. She didn't know how much longer she could press on. Her energy level teetered on empty.

"Someone's coming!" Raven shouted. "Hear it?"

But Amiya didn't hear anything; only her own tortured breaths, which had become like sobs, in between the crackle and thud of falling timber.

They burst out of the forest and into the bright headlights of an oncoming vehicle.

Amiya blinked, used her hand to protect her eyes against the sudden glare. The vehicle ground to a stop on the dirt road.

"Get in!" Grandpa Lee shouted.

Amiya didn't hesitate. She ran to the passenger side of the truck and flung open the door. She pushed in Ossie and Raven ahead of her, then she scrambled inside herself. It was a tight fit, the three of them practically sitting on top of one another, mashed up against Grandpa Lee, all of them so sweaty and hot the windows fogged up almost instantly.

"Hang tight." Grandpa Lee hit the accelerator. The truck jerked forward and bounced over bumps in the road, jostling them about.

Behind them, a tree exploded in a shower of golden sparks.

"He's still after us," Raven said.

Grandpa Lee grunted, poured on the speed. The truck's headlamps carved apart the darkness. Trees and foliage sped past. Amiya had a million questions for the man, but one sat uppermost in her mind.

"Have you seen Nick?" she asked.

"He's after us," Grandpa Lee said simply, with a nod toward the rearview mirror. "He took it from me, thought he was saving me. I can't let him wind up like me."

"He took *what* from you?" Amiya asked.

"The burden," he said. He gritted his teeth as he wrestled the truck around a bend in the road. "Someday he can tell you all about it, but right now we've got work to do."

"Hey, where we going?" Ossie asked.

"I brought some cans of kerosene in the flatbed," Grandpa Lee said. He grinned, a savage expression. "Wasn't sure I could manage to use 'em 'cause of the spell that came over me earlier . . . but we're going back to Westbrook and we're gonna burn down that damned place again."

57

Grandpa Lee drove the truck to the estate's front doors. Those doors hung open as Amiya and her group had left them. Some of the captives had wandered outdoors and milled in the front yard.

Many of them gaped at the vehicle, awestruck, as if it were a fiery chariot that had descended from the heavens.

"What good's it going to do to set it on fire when it gets made new every night?" Amiya asked Grandpa Lee.

"We've got to break the cycle," Grandpa Lee said. He slammed the truck into park. "It's like trying to untie a knot. We can't untie it, so we just gotta tear it all apart. Fire started the curse. Only fire can end it."

She didn't understand what he meant about a curse, but he seemed to have a depth of knowledge about the situation that surpassed everyone else's, and she questioned if he had known, all along, what had been going on back here. The possibility disturbed her.

But there was no time for such worries. The Overseer would turn up again, soon, and in the meantime, they had work to do.

She didn't want to dwell on the Overseer too much, either.

She forced open the passenger door. She and the others literally spilled out of the truck.

"If we're setting this place on fire," Raven said, "we've got to get everyone out of the house."

"I'll go with you," Ossie said. "We'll get everyone into the front yard, a good ways away from whatever fire you get going."

The two of them dashed inside the house through the front doorway.

Grandpa Lee lowered the truck's lift-gate and looked at Amiya. "Grab a couple cans of kerosene out the back here. You and me, we need to soak it down, every floor."

Amiya peered at the flatbed. Several gleaming metal cans of kerosene stood on the flatbed floor. It was enough of the flammable substance to set a fire on the property that would be visible for miles.

She slid two of the cans toward her, grabbed their handles, and lifted them out of the truck. It was like picking up two ten-pound dumbbells in each hand. She had been worn down from everything that had happened that day—the misadventures and terrors—but somehow, she summoned the strength to lug the kerosene toward the mansion's front steps.

"Matches." Grandpa Lee tossed her a box of matchsticks. "Don't wait around. Soon as you soak a room, light it up."

Amiya shuffled inside as fast as she could. The house staff, those who hadn't already gone outside, were in a state of chaos. Raven and Ossie were trying to convince them to leave, but Amiya saw people shaking their heads, crying, shouting disagreements.

"We're setting Westbrook on fire!" Amiya shouted, lifting a can of kerosene and waving it as if it were a flag. "Get out or you'll burn in here!"

Fear spread across their faces. Perhaps her warning would spur them into action.

Amiya hurried to the staircase, fuel sloshing with each step. It was a long journey to the third level, but she made it up there. She spun open a can and dribbled the clear, sharp-smelling fluid throughout the wide open area where she had first watched night come over the land.

Then she struck a match and set it ablaze.

The fire came instantly, like angry spirits rising from the floor. The intense heat baked the perspiration on her face. She hustled back down the staircase to the second floor.

The second floor contained all of the bedrooms and a bath, and she needed to saturate each one. Planning to work her way back from one end to the other, she began by opening the closed door at the termination of the long corridor.

It was a room she hadn't seen before, but she immediately recognized its purpose: Robert Westbrook's private quarters.

The décor was ostentatious: Persian area rugs with intricate designs; heavy maroon velvet draperies flanking the long double-sash windows; an immense four-post bed fashioned from mahogany, with gold highlights; overstuffed chairs with gold inlays; a glittering crystal chandelier; a fireplace spacious enough to roast a pig, alight with dancing flames.

Robert Westbrook stood in front of the fireplace. At her entrance, he turned.

"You've reconsidered my offer, eh, lady?" he asked.

Such a wave of shock washed over Amiya that she almost lost her grip on the kerosene can. Almost.

I slit his throat from ear to ear and watched him collapse. How can he be alive?

Although alive, his movements weren't as well-coordinated as before. His head appeared slightly out of sync with his neck, as if it had been soldered back onto his body by a blind craftsman. A faint red line marked where she had sliced his throat with the blade.

"I won't be such a gentleman this time, my lady," Westbrook said.

He flashed his shark's grin. He ambled toward her with jerky steps, like a poorly handled puppet.

Amiya grinned savagely. "I. Am. Not. Your. Lady!"

She thrust the can toward him, sending a shimmering arc of kerosene in his direction. The fluid spattered his face, the front of his tuxedo, and the surrounding rug. Westbrook scowled as if he'd tasted something foul.

Amiya lit a match and tossed it toward him.

He burst into flames like a tallow candle. He shrieked, and it was a terrible sound she'd never heard issue from anyone: like a screaming chorus of dying souls. Blindly, he stumbled into a wall. The wallpaper caught fire, crackling and smoking.

Amiya liberally saturated the rest of the bedroom and got out of there.

She went from one room to the next. Soon, she had emptied one can. She twisted open the other and continued to work through the vacant rooms. Foul-smelling black smoke poisoned the air. Flames crawled across the floors, walls, and ceilings as she backed toward the head of the staircase.

Downstairs, she heard someone scream. She turned, sweat dripping from her brow.

The Overseer had arrived. He loomed at the bottom of the staircase. All around him, flames danced, and smoke twisted about him in serpent-like tendrils.

Amiya dropped the kerosene, put her hand to her mouth.

It was Nick . . . but it wasn't. He wore the clothing of a prior era, and the clothes fit his slender frame as if they had been tailored especially for him. But the true difference was in his eyes. He looked at her as if he didn't recognize her at all. The soul of the man she loved had to be buried somewhere in that body, but it was hidden behind a mask of hatred and rage.

"You must be marked," he said.

He lifted the glowing branding iron.

He ascended the steps toward her.

58

The woman would be a fine addition to his collection. The Overseer thought he needed to mind where he marked her, as he didn't want to spoil her beauty, but mark her he would, and then he would turn her over to the master for his carnal pleasure.

She stood frozen at the top of the staircase. Curtains of flames rippled and flapped at her back. The growing conflagration concerned the Overseer. He had once perished in such a fire at the plantation. He had risen again . . . but only with the assistance of the ancient ones, the silent watchers who fed on the pain that he so skillfully dispensed.

The woman, however, unmarked and free, was so irresistible that he set aside his caution and ascended toward her.

Tears spilled down her soot-covered cheeks. Her crying gave the Overseer a charge of pleasure.

"You will never run away," the Overseer said.

As the Overseer reached for her, she struck a match and thrust her hand toward him. She had some sort of item in her fist. Something with a glowing wick.

She stuck it into his jacket.

"I love you, Nick," she said.

59

Burying that sizzling, hand-crafted firecracker in Nick's jacket was an act of pure desperation on Amiya's part. She didn't know what it would accomplish, if anything. At best, she hoped it might provide a distraction to allow her to escape the burning mansion.

"I love you, Nick," she had said, and had never meant the declaration more than she did then.

At the mention of his name, dull recognition flickered in his eyes. He stopped his hand, the branding iron so close to her cheek that she could feel its flesh-searing heat.

"Babe?" he asked, as if waking from a dream.

The firecracker exploded with a searing flash of light and sound. Nick's eyes went wide, his consciousness fully restored—but he lost his balance on the steps. The branding iron dropped from his fingers. Nick tumbled like a log down the long spiral staircase.

Praying that he would be okay, Amiya hurried down the steps after him. Grandpa Lee came around the corner of the newel post at the bottom of the staircase. The old man was drenched in sweat, and it looked as if flames had singed his beard.

Both of them went to Nick. Nick lay on the last few steps, head turned to the side. He wore his normal clothes again, but there was a dark spot on his abdomen, a stain of blood and charred clothing.

"No." Amiya touched his head.

"Come on now, son," Grandpa Lee said, crouched next to him. He coughed, the smoke growing thicker. "It's not your time."

Nick breathed—and gagged. Amiya cradled his head in her hands and helped him to sit up.

"Are you okay?" she asked. "I'm so sorry, Nick. I didn't want to hurt you but—"

"It's okay." His voice was raspy. "Think we ought to get out of here, guys."

Amiya and Grandpa Lee helped Nick stand. The house was falling apart around them. Timbers collapsed from the ceiling. Draperies billowed and snapped with flames. Clouds of black, suffocating smoke wafted through the rooms.

Nick hung his arm across Amiya's shoulders. Grandpa Lee helped to steady his grandson, and turned away from them.

"Hey," Nick said. "Grandpa?"

"I'm taking on the burden, son," Grandpa Lee said. "You kids get on out of here now."

"Wait!" Amiya said.

But Grandpa Lee ignored both of them. He raced to the staircase. He picked up the branding iron from where it had fallen onto a step.

Amiya didn't know if the churning smoke had distorted her vision, but once he put his hands on that terrible tool, he was no longer the beloved grandfather who had been so sweet to her. He transformed, in an instant, into the fearsome Overseer.

And she saw huge, distorted faces gathered around Grandpa Lee, their features formed from the billowing smoke and flames, their hungry mouths open in shouts of an unknown language, demanding final payment in exchange for freedom.

The ancient, evil entities, a primitive part of her mind whispered, and cold, raw terror came over her. *The powers behind it all . . .*

She tore her gaze away and looked at Nick, and from the fear flashing in his eyes, she realized he saw them, too.

Grandpa Lee looked back at both of them, once, and it was an image that would be seared in Amiya's brain for the rest of her life: a man of two minds, one of love, one of hate.

He pressed the branding iron against his own chest.

And, roaring, he charged into the flames.

60

The entire estate was on fire.

Amiya at his side, Nick leaned against Grandpa Lee's truck a safe distance away from the flames and watched Westbrook burn. Raven and Ossie were nearby, as were many others —the captives who had wanted to escape. Not all of them had taken the opportunity to leave.

Like his granddad, some had willfully remained inside.

"I don't understand what happened." Amiya sniffled, wiped tears from her face with the heel of her hand. "For a while, you were *him*, that terrible man, and at the end it was your grandfather. How?"

Shaking his head, Nick pulled in a ragged breath. "I barely remember any of it. It's like a dream that you mostly forget when you wake up. You can recall only fragments of it. All I can clearly remember is . . . I wanted to help my granddad."

"And he wanted to help you," Amiya said softly. She squeezed his hand as if sensing he needed reassurance. "He wanted to help all of us."

The burn above Nick's kidney would be a permanent reminder

of his grandfather's sacrifice. The pain was severe and would require medical treatment, but he was in no hurry to leave.

He needed to mind the fire.

The flames had spread to the plantation's supporting structures: the barn, warehouse, and other buildings. All of it needed to burn, Nick had realized. Grandpa Lee, in his wisdom, had known that the only way to start anew was to destroy it all.

Soon, Raven and Ossie wandered over. Both of them wore tentative smiles, and appeared hesitant to speak, as though they feared the answers to their questions.

Maybe they're afraid of me, Nick thought. They must have seen what he had become, though as he had told Amiya, he recalled only bits and pieces of the experience.

"Will we be able to leave now?" Raven asked. "People are getting restless. They want to try to go home."

"Your mark is gone," Amiya said. She touched Raven's face, brushed back strands of her hair. "Not just faded. Completely gone."

"Really?" Tears shone in Raven's eyes. She looked at Nick for confirmation. "You think I could cross over the bridge?"

"Why don't we give it a try?" Nick said. "This fire will be burning all night. I've got to tend to it for a while, but you all don't need to stay here in the meantime. You can go home. Someone needs to tell the field hands, too. Everyone needs to go."

"Let's be sure we can get out first," Ossie said.

Nick got behind the wheel of his granddad's pickup truck. Amiya squeezed in beside him. Raven, Ossie, and several of the others either packed into the cabin or climbed into the truck's empty flatbed.

The key wasn't in the ignition. Nick remembered that his granddad usually kept one tucked underneath the sun visor. He flipped down the weathered flap.

He discovered two items: a set of keys and a business-size manila envelope with his name on the front, inscribed in his grandfather's careful handwriting.

People were packed in the truck, hot, sweaty, and eager to go, but Nick couldn't delay. He tore open the envelope.

"What is it?" Amiya peered over his shoulder.

"My grandfather's will." Nick skimmed the legalese in the vehicle's dim interior light. His heart pounded. "All of the property, everything, he left to me."

"I'm sorry, Nick," Amiya said.

"Yeah, me, too." Nick blinked away a tear. He started the truck's engine. "Let's get all of you folks on your way. I think you've waited long enough to go home."

They crossed over the bridge together.

61

One week later…

    Nick closed the door to the meeting room.

    Omar and Shango sat at the square conference table. Shango's bodyguard, Wanda, stood behind her boss, massaging her scarred knuckles.

Nick strolled to the head of the table, a laptop case dangling from his shoulder. His movements were slowed a bit by the bandage covering his burn wound. But he didn't take a chair.

"Thank all of you for coming here to the company headquarters this morning, on short notice," Nick said. "We're here to discuss the future of Legacy Nutrition."

A frown crinkled Shango's features. Omar stared at Nick, mouth agape; he was Nick's business partner, but Nick hadn't given him any clue about the purpose of this meeting.

"I'll get to the point," Nick said. "I'm done with Legacy Nutrition. All my shares, all of my patented formulations, belong to you guys now. I'm not selling them. I'm *giving* them to you, no strings attached."

"What the hell's the matter with you?" Omar asked. "We're partners, man. You can't drop out like that."

"We're on the same page there, brother," Shango said, nodding toward Omar. He straightened his jacket. "You're a major piece of this empire we're building. You don't get to decide when you're out. I decide."

"You don't." Nick placed the laptop case on the table. "All of my formulations are on the laptop's hard drive in this bag. If you need help with them, I'm sure you can find another chemist willing to work for you at the right price."

"You, and him"—Shango pointed from Nick to Omar—"owe me a significant amount of money."

"I don't owe you anything. There's a letter in this bag stipulating the cancellation of my ownership in the company. I'm done here, folks."

Nick turned on his heel and strolled across the room. Shango made an angry gesture toward Wanda and the bodyguard moved to block Nick's path.

Her lips twisted into a menacing snarl. She raised one hand into a clenched fist that could have shattered his jaw.

Nick only stared at her. For a long moment, their gazes were locked.

The fighter must have seen something in his eyes, perhaps a glimpse of the monster Nick had once been, even if only for a fleeting instant, because she lowered her gaze and slid aside.

No one else attempted to stop him.

Outside the building, Nick climbed into his truck. He didn't start the ignition, didn't grab the steering wheel. The gravity of what he had accomplished in those few momentous minutes came over him like a sugar high, and he allowed himself a short time to luxuriate in his delight, trembling like a kid, too wound up to do anything.

Once he felt ready to talk, he called Amiya on his cell phone.

"How did things go?" she asked.

"It's done," he said. "It went about as I expected: they were pissed."

"They'll get over it," she said. "So. What are you going to do now?"

"I think I'm going to make dinner plans tonight with a certain special lady," he said.

"Is that so?" He could hear the smile in her voice.

"We've got a lot to talk about, she and I," he said. "We've got to talk about our future together as husband and wife."

"Well, I don't want to give anything away," she said, punctuating her words with a light laugh. "But I think she'd enjoy that very much."

HEAR MORE FROM BRANDON

ABOUT BRANDON MASSEY

Brandon Massey was born June 9, 1973, and grew up in Zion, Illinois. He lives with his family near Atlanta, Georgia, where he is at work on his next novel. Visit his web site at www.brandon-massey.com for the latest news on his upcoming books.

Printed in Dunstable, United Kingdom

71442370R00150